HONEYMAKER'S SON

ALSO BY RAY HOGAN

JACKMAN'S WOLF
CONGER'S WOMAN
MAN WITHOUT A GUN

HONEYMAKER'S SON

RAY HOGAN

DOUBLEDAY & COMPANY, INC.

GARDEN CITY, NEW YORK

1975

All of the characters in this book
are fictitious, and any resemblance
to actual persons, living or dead,
is purely coincidental.

Library of Congress Cataloging in Publication Data

Hogan, Ray, 1908–
  Honeymaker's son.

  I. Title.
PZ4.H716Ho [PS3558.03473]   813'.5'4
ISBN 0-385-03124-6
Library of Congress Catalog Card Number 74–12857

for—
      Mike and Darleen Hogan
                   in Studio City

Tom Honeymaker, moving across the hard-pack lying between the ranch house and the wagon shed where he was repairing the buckboard, paused. Swiping at the sweat collected on his forehead, he stared at the rider entering the gate. It was Murcer, one of the cowhands. He was leading a buckskin horse.

Pearly Quinn, the cook, peeling potatoes in the shade of a cottonwood just outside the kitchen door, squinted into the glare. "Who's that?"

A coldness settled over Tom. The body of a man was draped over the saddle of the horse. "It's Pa," he said, starting forward.

Murcer pulled to a halt in the center of the yard, his long face sober. "Found him up on the ledge. Dead; shot in the back."

For a full minute Tom stared at the limp, lifeless figure and then, jaw set, he stepped forward, lifted the body off the buckskin, and shouldering it, carried it into the house. Others were now coming up, asking questions of Murcer and following slowly in Honeymaker's wake.

Tom entered the bedroom, laid his parent on the bed, and stepped back, vaguely aware of Quinn and Murcer, of old Manuel, who looked after the yard chores, and several more hired hands gathering around the doorway.

"All hell won't hold back the wolves around here now," Quinn said heavily. "We all best get set for trouble."

Let it come, Tom thought, turning about to face the men. He knew he could expect little else; Burl Honeymaker had spent a lifetime making enemies in the Cibola Valley country and they all would be moving in now to reclaim the pound of flesh he had exacted from them. Honeymaker had built a mighty ranch empire at the expense of everyone else, including his own son, and now restitution would begin.

"Any sign of who could've done it?" Tom asked, centering his attention on Murcer.

Tall, with dark hair and eyes, a square-cut jaw and thick shoulders, he looked much like his father, but there the similarity ended. Where Burl Honeymaker was a driving, ruthless force riding roughshod over all, Tom was inclined to reason and patience—characteristics Burl had publicly and scornfully on many occasions designated as weaknesses.

The puncher shook his head. "Didn't see nobody. I was over in the brush, near the line, chousing strays. Heard a rifle shot and rode over to see what it was about. Found your pa just laying there dead."

"Was it over in them big rocks, by the buttes?" It was Jim Heston, one of the older hands. Like Quinn, Gabe Archer, and Tularosa, a vaquero, he had worked on the Diamond G almost from the day Burl Honeymaker had branded his first beef.

"Right up on the top," Murcer said.

Pearly Quinn clucked. "Was a kind of special place for him. Told me once he could see dang nigh to the south corner of his range from there—was it a clear day."

A long silence followed, and then Ed Davis, one of the

new punchers, demanded in an angry voice: "Well, what're we going to do about it—just stand here?"

Tom felt their close attention. They were watching him, waiting, forming their judgments. Not one of them believed he could fill his father's boots, that was certain—but they would want to be sure.

"Nothing," he said flatly. "Leastwise—"

"What?" Davis shouted. "Well, by God, I'm for mounting a posse and going gunning for whoever done it! I'll get word to Bill Jacks—he worshiped that there pa of yours, and we'll—"

"Forget it," Tom broke in calmly. "Whoever shot Pa is miles from here now and looking for him would be a waste of time. . . . And while we're talking, best you get something straight. I'm running this ranch now and it'll be me giving the orders. Maybe some of you don't think I'm big enough for the job but that counts for nothing. That clear?"

Davis shrugged. "You ain't nothing like old Burl," he said bluntly. "Don't see how you can."

Anger pulled at the corners of Honeymaker's mouth, narrowed his eyes. "Your opinion's not worth a damn to me," he said. "And whether you keep on riding for the Diamond G means even less. You can draw your time whenever you want. . . . Same goes for every man working on this ranch. Like to know if you've got that straight, too."

Davis scuffed the dirt with the toe of his boot. "Yeh, reckon I have—"

There was little conviction in the man's tone. Tom studied him briefly, shifted his attention to the others.

"Want one of you to ride into Rimrock, tell the deputy. And we'll need a coffin."

"Me and Gabe can knock one together," Murcer volunteered. "Expect you're planning to bury him out there on the hill, next to your ma."

Tom nodded. As the only son of Burl Honeymaker, he knew he should be feeling pangs of grief at his death, but the years of disaffection and incompatibility that lay between them were as a wall of rock and he was utterly unmoved.

"I'll put Manuel to digging the grave," Archer said.

There was a shuffling of feet as the men, with the exception of Quinn, turned to leave. Tom felt the old cook's hand on his arm.

"Coming sudden like this I know—"

"Makes no difference. Just happens he was my pa. Hell, I hardly knew him."

"He was that kind. Reckon there weren't nobody, 'cepting your ma, that ever did. But he was square and he was honest, even if he was a mite highhanded—you just keep remembering that."

"What I remember was that he never had any use for me—and because of him we had no friends."

"It was his natural way, him being a loner like he was. But what he got, he got hisself, without no tail-kissing and backslapping. He done the work of ten men building this place up to what it is, and he'll be expecting you to hang on to it—every dang bit of it."

Like Ed Davis, Pearly Quinn was having his doubts, too, right along with the others. Tom glanced at the slack figure on the bed. His shoulders stirred faintly.

"Don't expect me to be another Burl Honeymaker. What has to be done will be done my way, not his."

Quinn looked down, wagged his head slowly. In the hard sunlight his leathery skin took on dull ruddiness.

"Meaning no offense, son, but pussyfooting around ain't going to get the job done—specially when it comes to holding on to the Rinconada. You show one sign of backing up and Kanin and Mayo and Gus McNabb, and plenty of others'll move right in on you!"

"If they ever get any Honeymaker range it'll be because I let them have it, not because they took it," Tom said evenly. "You mind seeing to Pa?"

Quinn shrugged. "Sure not. . . . Whyn't you go on over to my kitchen, get yourself some coffee. You aim to hold up on the burying any?"

"What for? Who'd come?"

"Reckon you're right," Quinn said, not missing the edge of bitterness in the younger man's tone. And then as Tom turned for the door, Quinn added, "I'll call you when I'm done."

Honeymaker stepped out into the yard, crossed slowly to the cookshack. Entering, he helped himself to the coffee simmering on the back of the big Detroit range and sat down at the table, big hands locked about the crockery cup filled to the brim with black liquid. The rap of hammers in the barn and the thud of a pick and the scrape of a shovel on the hillside nearby indicated that Archer and Murcer and old Manuel were busy at their part of the preparations.

The full impact of the situation was beginning now to seep into Tom's consciousness. His pa was dead. It was a thought that would require some getting used to. Why,

5

only a few hours earlier he had watched him ride out after giving the day's orders to Bill Jacks, the ranch foreman—and now they were getting ready to put him into the ground and cover him over with dirt!

In all of his nineteen years Tom had never given the possibility of such any consideration; it had simply never occurred to him. Burl Honeymaker had been like the land, like the great, shining palisades that towered over the valley—each would endure forever.

That had proven untrue. Burl was gone and now he was the owner of the vast Diamond G with all its land and cattle—and the lush Rinconada. . . . The Rinconada . . . it had been a source of hate and contention for as long as he could recall, a time in which, with each passing year, the tension and resentment concerning its ownership had mounted steadily.

A broad, deep canyon, it lay as a green pocket along the upper end of the Honeymaker range; a place of sweet grass, clear water springs, and steep rock and brush-studded walls that shielded it from the hot winds of summer, the frigid blasts of winter. And it lay untouched.

Gathered in by Burl Honeymaker in those first critical years during which he was increasing his holdings by rule of possessory right, he had from the start determined that it would be his reserve, his ace in the hole, should the time ever come when nature or misfortune compelled him to seek grazing for his beef elsewhere than on his usual range. Only then would he drive his herds into that virgin paradise he had named the Rinconada.

That day had never come—and likely never would, Tom had long ago decided, for by reason of its sprawling extent coupled with the judicious use of its grass yield, there was

6

always more than ample grazing for Diamond G stock. Likely Burl was aware of that also, but it was contrary to his make-up ever to give up even a single square foot of his hard-won land, needed by him or not.

Maintaining that stubborn stance had not been easy. Pressure on him to relinquish the Rinconada increased continually, most of it coming from Henry Kanin to the south, McNabb and Con Mayo to the north—all ranchers like himself but unlike him in that they were withering from lack of more and better range. And there were others in similar plight to the west.

Violence had marked the passage of time on many occasions. Twice there had been attempts to move herds into the Rinconada in the belief that possession would alter ownership. Honeymaker's foreman, Bill Jacks, an ex-lawman, and the gun-handy crew he had assembled to protect Diamond G's interests saw to it that the cattle never reached their intended destination.

Night riders often coursed the range, beef was wantonly slaughtered and left for the coyotes and buzzards; line shacks were looted and burned, grass fires ignited, men shot and killed or crippled, and all through the deadly game of strike and retaliate Burl Honeymaker had stood, a rugged monolith bearing the fury of storms, surrendering nothing and utterly impervious to the ever rising clamor of hate swirling about him.

That was his heritage, Tom thought, and the role he would be expected to assume. The old hates would now be transferred from father to son and the war would continue, perhaps even intensify as Kanin and the others sought to test him, see if he—

"Tom—"

7

Honeymaker glanced up as Pearly Quinn halted in the doorway. He noticed then that the hammering in the barn and the digging on the hill had ceased.

"He's all ready."

Tom nodded, got to his feet, and moved toward the older man. "Let's get it over with," he said.

2

It was shortly after noon when Deputy Sheriff Gable, accompanied by the cowhand who had gone to fetch him, rode into the yard at Diamond G. The lawman was elderly —well up in his sixties—and once had served a stint as a marshal in one of the Kansas trail towns. Ramrod straight, his snow-white hair down to shoulder length, mustache full and always neatly combed, he was a stern figure in wide-brimmed hat and slate-gray whipcord.

"Would've got here sooner," he drawled as Tom came out onto the porch of the ranch house to meet him. "Happens I had a few chores to attend."

"Figures," Honeymaker said coolly. Gable had long ago made it clear that he stood with the other ranchers in the Cibola valley.

The deputy studied him thoughtfully for a long breath. Then, "You got any ideas who bushwhacked him?"

Tom glanced toward the bunkhouse where a dozen or so of the crew were gathered around Bill Jacks. As far as the foreman was concerned Burl Honeymaker's killer was either Henry Kanin, Con Mayo, Gus McNabb—or an employee of theirs, and it was his opinion that a vigilante raid should be made on each immediately and a full measure of vengeance taken.

"No," Tom said, shaking his head. "I called the men in,

9

talked to them all. Nobody's seen any strangers on the range—or anybody from one of the other ranches, either."

"Was somebody for sure," Gable murmured, his own attention now shifting to Bill Jacks and the others. "Expect I'd best have a look at the body."

"Too late for that. Buried him this morning. . . . He'd been shot in the back if that's what you're wondering about."

"That's what I was wondering about," Gable said agreeably. "Had he been robbed? Could've been some drifter—"

"Still had a hundred dollars or so in gold eagles and silver in his pockets." Tom paused, looking squarely at the older man. "Reckon we both know who it had to be, Deputy—somebody right here in the valley carrying a big grudge."

"Probably—and that covers a powerful lot of folks. Burl Honeymaker didn't have many men around who'd lag for him—if any."

"Maybe not," Tom snapped, unexpectedly finding himself coming to the defense of his father, "but they were the ones that made him like he was—having to fight all the time for what was his against Kanin and—"

"You accusing Henry Kanin of killing him?"

"Don't be trying to make out what I'm saying means more than it does," Honeymaker replied tautly, anger rising higher. "We both know he's one who'd have a reason."

"You talking about him needing more range and wanting the Rinconada?"

"Just what I am—him and Mayo and McNabb to mention the main ones."

"Well, they've got themselves a problem—a real bad one, no doubt. Point is you could help them out and put an end to all the trouble around here now."

"By handing over the Rinconada to them?"

"That's the answer. You ain't using it—never have. Not right for a—"

"Forget it, Deputy. Nothing's changed where the Rinconada's concerned."

Gable's jaw tightened. "That mean you aim to let things stand right where they was when your pa was alive?"

"Figure to run the ranch same as he did."

The lawman's shoulders twitched. "Could be you're in for a surprise. You ain't Burl Honeymaker—and keeping that pack of gunnies hanging around," he said, jerking a thumb toward Jacks and the men clustered around him, "ain't going to make it so."

"I'll look after my crew," Tom said quietly, "you take care of your job. Law requires that a murder be reported. I've done that. Up to you to try and track down the killer, not waste time telling me how to run my ranch."

"Somebody ought've taught you some respect for your elders, boy," Gable said stiffly. "I'll do my job, but it happens it's also up to me to keep the peace around here and from the way your hackles're standing up, I can see I'll have to keep an eye on you."

"Be no trouble around here far as the Diamond G is concerned."

The lawman spat. "Hell, that's a fool thing to say! You know same as me that with your pa in his grave this country's going to bust wide open unless—"

"Unless I give in to what they want? I'm not about to, and if you just happen to bump into any of them you can tell them so for me. . . . You going to put in any time looking for the man who killed my pa?"

Gable bobbed curtly. "I am, same as I would if it was

somebody else. And if I find him he'll go to jail and stand trial, same as anybody else."

"Making no difference who he is?"

"Makes no difference."

"All I want to hear. . . . I'm riding over to where it happened. You're welcome to come along."

The deputy turned, stepped down off the porch, and moved toward his horse. "Can't see no need. That bushwhacker wouldn't still be hanging around there, and I ain't apt to find anything that'd help."

"Suit yourself," Tom said, as the lawman went stiffly onto his saddle.

He had done what was required of him: advised the proper authority of the murder, but he had known in advance that he could expect little help. If his pa's killer was to be found it would probably be up to him personally to do it.

Silent, he watched Gable wheel his buckskin about and head toward the distant gate. For a time he stood there, gazing at the lawman, and then, picking up his hat, he started for the corral to get his horse.

Gable was likely right about the futility of looking over the scene where the murder had taken place, but he would do so, anyway. Besides, there were a few things he needed to think over and get straightened out in his mind.

3

Emory Justin, his lined face sober, stood at the window of his store and literally watched the news of Burl Honeymaker's death spread along Rimrock's main street. From door to door, person to person, it made its swift rounds. By dark every one in the valley would have the word.

A slight tremor shook the merchant. Ordinarily a calm, deliberate man given to deep thought and consideration, he was having forebodings now as to the future. Burl Honeymaker had been bushwhacked—murdered; such was tantamount to hurling a flaming torch into a tinder-dry brush pile.

The uneasy peace the Cibola Valley had known since Henry Kanin, Con Mayo, and to a lesser degree, Gus McNabb, had taken it in mind to challenge Honeymaker and spread their holdings would not stand for long now. Burl had been a brake on their ambitions, a clamp on the lid that held them in line; with him out of the picture anything could happen.

No one would figure Tom Honeymaker strong enough to withstand the pressures the coming hours would unleash upon him. He'd be powerless to ward off the wolves who would come rushing in determined to slice up and devour the vast Diamond G spread. They'd simply ignore him— hell, he was only a boy! Boy? Come to think of it he must be nineteen or twenty years old at that. Justin reckoned that it was the fact that Burl Honeymaker had never made much of his son, refusing always to let him take a hand in matters pertaining to the ranch that gave folks the idea he was still a boy.

It was too bad. Tom was going to be caught in the middle, made to pay a price for his father's actions; there was no question of that. The question was, who among the big three ranchers would win out? Who would prove the most ruthless and therefore the strongest?

Would it be Henry Kanin with his big crew of men and cash enough to buy just about anything he pleased, including influence and the support of many under obligation to him? Only Burl Honeymaker had been powerful enough to buck him, laugh in his face. Was Kanin now going to have the last laugh?

Or would it be loud-talking, hard-driving Con Mayo? He was the relentless kind, generally got what he went after—one way or another. A stillness settled over Emory Justin as a darker thought came to him; could Mayo have had something to do with Honeymaker's death? He was a man capable of such once the necessity for the act became apparent to him. But he reckoned that went for Kanin, too, and possibly even McNabb.

Gus McNabb, the quiet-spoken Scotsman—he could turn out to be the one who picked up all the chips. Gus fooled just about everybody. He never raised his voice, never lifted a hand in anger or displayed impatience, but of the three big ranch owners he probably was by far the cleverest and therefore the most dangerous.

McNabb would not be one who'd move in on Tom

Honeymaker like a spring flood, using force and flaming guns if need be. He'd do it quietly, testing each footstep, probing, feeling his way, but doing all steadily, surely. He was a man who seldom made a mistake.

You could throw all of the rule books away now, however, Justin decided grimly, his eyes settling on Kanin just then emerging from Sisto Salazar's livery stable. Things would happen fast and none of the three could be counted on to do the expected—only the opportune.

Sighing, the store owner turned away from the window. He probably was about as close to being a friend as Burl Honeymaker had, and that because the rancher knew him to be a man who kept his mouth shut, minded his own business strictly, and never offered any advice. He wondered now if, out of respect to Burl, he should have a talk with Tom and see if he could help in some way.

Tom would stand no chance against the likes of Mayo, Kanin, or Gus McNabb, all of whom were undoubtedly planning their first move. . . . The jasper who'd bushwhacked Burl Honeymaker didn't realize the depth of the fury he'd unleashed in the Cibola Valley when he cut down the rancher. Or did he?

Henry Kanin had been in the office of Deputy Sheriff Luke Gable filing a complaint against a cowpuncher who'd worked for him a few days and then moved on, neglecting to pay for the horse he was riding at the time. It wasn't that the horse was particularly valuable; it was simply that you couldn't allow a thing like that to pass; it would give the other hired hands ideas. . . . Fellow's name was Trux Galvan. . . . Pass the word along to lawmen in all of the surrounding towns to be on the lookout and haul the bastard in if he showed up. Charge him with being a horse thief.

Deputy Gable had been taking it all down, working his pencil laboriously over a sheet of paper, undoubtedly cursing silently as he thought about all the letters he would now have to write, when the rider from the Diamond G walked in, halted before the littered, dusty desk.

"Sheriff, Tom Honeymaker sent me to fetch you. His pa's been shot dead."

Kanin drew up slowly. He was a lean, tall man in his early fifties, had graying brown hair and small, sharp eyes. A look of satisfaction had spread across his narrow features.

"Shot dead?" the lawman had echoed. "You know who done it?"

"Nope, sure don't. Reckon nobody does. Charley Murcer found him laying near the buttes."

Gable had frowned. "I'm right busy just now. It'll be a while."

"Tom was saying he'd like for you to come right out—"

"Can only do one damned thing at a time!" the old lawman had snapped.

At that point Kanin had turned, stepped out into the street, and made his way leisurely to Sudreth's Buckhorn Saloon. There, calling for his private bottle, he had taken it to a table in the back and settled down to think about the changes that now would come.

Burl Honeymaker, the thorn that had always been in his side, the stubborn detriment, the hindrance to all of the plans he had for the Box K and his son Joe, had at last been removed. Now he could make all of those grand dreams impatiently clamoring inside his head for so long come true.

He'd finally have the Rinconada, and possessing it, he could proceed with his long cherished idea of moving into it a large herd of prime, selected cattle, sealing them off, and breeding up a good strain of steers—animals that would run heavy to beef but would still be rugged enough to withstand the trail drive to a shipping point without a noticeable loss of tallow.

The Rinconada plus maybe the upper third of Honeymaker's land to permit easy access to the basin was all he'd need, and with it the load on the rest of his range would be relieved. Taking another swing at the bottle, he smiled in satisfaction. He'd waited—and worked—a long time for this day. It was a good feeling knowing it had come at last.

Con Mayo, working the brush in the upper canyons of his Walking M range for strays, pulled into the shade of a young cottonwood at sight of the approaching rider, and hooking one leg over the horn of his saddle, brushed his hat to the back of his head and spat. A short, vigorous man with a hard-set face, he prided himself on being a working rancher and not one of those who directed operations from a rocking chair. Nevertheless, he was glad his brother Hod was coming to lend a hand. It was going to be too much for one man now.

"That ain't no surprise," he said with a shrug to the cowpuncher, who, after nodding his greeting, advised him of Burl Honeymaker's death. "That sonofabitch's had it coming to him for years."

The rider grinned, cocked his head to one side. "Yeh, I reckon there won't be much moaning and groaning at his burying."

"I hated that bastard, same as he hated me," Mayo rumbled on, seemingly unhearing. "Always been that way."

The puncher drew out his makings and worked up a quirley. "Was a mean old range bull for sure. Once took a shot at me for short-cutting slanchwise across a corner of his land. All I was doing—riding across."

"He was that kind—downright unreasonable. Man nobody could talk to, and he'd as soon tromp you into the ground as look at you. . . . Done just that to a-plenty."

The rider nodded solemnly, fired a match with a thumbnail. Cupping the small flame to the slim cylinder of tobacco hanging from his lips, he sucked deeply, filled his lungs with smoke and let it trickle out of his nostrils.

"I reckon all hell's going to start popping around here now—"

"Can bet your bottom dollar on it!" Mayo cut in, scrubbing at the whiskers on his chin. "Every man jack in this valley's going to be after a piece of Honeymaker range. And me—I'm going to be right at the head of the line. I've been working for this day for a long time and anybody tries pushing in ahead of me is going to get a hide full of lead."

"What if this here Tom Honeymaker ain't of a mind to turn loose of any land?"

"He ain't man enough to stop me! Cows of mine are finding the grazing mighty slim on my range, and I aim to change that. That Rinconada canyon ain't never had stock run on it. By this time next month it's going to be chock full of my beef—can bet your bottom dollar on that, too!"

Word of Burl Honeymaker's death reached Angus McNabb through his daughter Ellie. She had been in Mrs. Macy's Dress Shop when the report, leaked from Deputy Gable's office, had swept through the town.

McNabb, slouched in his favorite rocker on the front porch of their house, came to attention. Outwardly nothing ever hurried the old Scotsman, but within him furiously churning machinery could be set in motion instantly should it be a matter of personal importance and the occasion warrant.

Removing the blackened briar from between his clenched teeth, he nodded slightly. "So . . . They know who done it?"

Ellie, leafing through a back issue of a *Godey's* she had borrowed from Mrs. Macy, shook her head. "The deputy was just going out there to try and find out."

"Like as not they'll never know," the rancher murmured, thrusting the stem of the pipe back between his teeth and reaching for a match. Pausing, he added: "You and the Honeymaker boy—you were in school together, weren't you?"

"Yes, Papa. You've asked me that before. Tom and I were in school at the same time. No, he never paid much attention to me, and no, I was never sweet on him."

Expression unchanging, McNabb struck the match, held the small flame to the bowl of his pipe, and puffed it into life.

"A pity," he murmured, settling back in the chair.

Ellie, the pale azure dress she wore setting off well her dusky skin, dark hair, and blue eyes, closed the magazine and smiled down at her father.

"Not that I would've objected, mind you," she said. "I always liked Tom. He's a lot nicer than that Joe Kanin . . . handsomer, too," she finished, and moving on by him, entered the house.

McNabb puffed methodically on his pipe, gaze lost on the distant Jackrabbit Mountains. It certainly would have been fine had there been something between young Honey-maker and Ellie; with Burl out of the way it would make it easy to get a lot of things straightened out, having an in-side track, but there was no use thinking about it—and there wasn't time enough now to get something started between them . . . he'd just have to do the best he could, otherwise.

It would be smart to ride by and see Tom. After all they were neighbors—leastwise he was the closest; and with Burl dead it could be the boy would welcome a friendly pat on the back and a little advice from an older man. He'd let drop a word or two about being real careful where Henry Kanin and Con Mayo and others like them were concerned. Maybe it would be a good idea to sort of sug-gest they kind of line up together, make a stand against all comers. The way Burl had always treated the boy, keeping him down, never letting him take a hand in running the ranch and such, he was probably pretty much at sea and not sure what he ought to be doing next.

Gus reckoned he'd best get at that right soon, too; he could figure on Kanin and Mayo both not letting any grass grow under their feet. They'd be thinking the same way he was, and if he got to dillydallying around one of them would cut him out for sure.

4

Riding slowly through the grove of squat piñon trees flanking the low hills to the southeast, Tom Honeymaker began to organize his thoughts and consider the future. The hours and events since daylight had come and gone so swiftly that he had done little more than meet each moment as it presented itself; now it was time to make decisions.

There were two things he must do: run down his father's killer and see him brought to justice, and take steps to not only protect the ranch—his ranch—but head off if possible the trouble that was now sure to come. And there would be trouble, he could be certain of that. Regardless of who had sighted down a rifle barrel and squeezed off the shot that had killed Burl Honeymaker, Kanin and Mayo and probably Gus McNabb would grasp the opportunity to move in on Diamond G range and cut out whatever portion they felt would satisfy their needs. With Burl Honeymaker alive such had been an impossibility; now that he was dead they would be convinced that it could be accomplished with little effort.

Again he wondered about his three principal neighbors and the likelihood of one of them being behind the killing. That Kanin had far-reaching ambitions was undeniable; he had the largest ranch in both acreage and stock in the

Cibola Valley, but he wanted still more. Was that desire strong enough to kill?

Tom's pa had always stood in Kanin's way, Tom knew, and thus there had always been hostility between them. From the very beginning, Kanin, moving onto the land that was to become the Box K, had coveted the Rinconada and had tried every means to obtain it.

He had even gone to the Territorial Land Office, petitioned the officials to force Honeymaker into relinquishing his claim to the land on the grounds that it was not in use. The move had failed. The authorities had advised him there was no way they could compel the owner of an area to sell or lease his property if he did not wish to do so.

It could have been Henry Kanin, or someone hired by him. He had reason—but so did Gus McNabb. The Scotsman's Circle A lay next to Diamond G's north line, and while Gus had often flatly expressed his need and desire for more grazing, it was usually with much less fervor than that displayed by Kanin or his adjacent neighbor, Mayo.

Too, it was known that McNabb was being prodded constantly by Mayo to keep at Honeymaker, hopefully to persuade him to release claim on some of his land, including the Rinconada, for their mutual use. To obtain his own end, Mayo undoubtedly was seeking to take advantage of the lesser degree of enmity existing between McNabb and the hard-fisted owner of the Diamond G; true, he would have to drive his stock across McNabb land to reach the Rinconada and the range fronting it, but he probably felt he would have no problems striking an agreement with the Scotsman.

Gus McNabb was the least likely suspect, Tom thought, as he pressed on toward the rocky ledges, now visible above the scrub growth. But Con Mayo was something else; the possibility that he was involved in the murder was on equal footing with the likelihood that Henry Kanin was guilty.

Of course it could be some other rancher, one having felt the crush of Burl Honeymaker's heel, and brooding over what he considered an injustice, had righted that past wrong by taking matters into his own hands. It might have been an old and long forgotten enemy—and there was the chance that it was some dismissed hired hand with a festering grudge. His pa had shown no favoritism when it came to spreading ill will and accumulating hate; Tom was well aware of that fact.

But such probabilities were at the bottom of the list shaping up in Tom Honeymaker's mind. The death of his father had come about because of the Rinconada and other surplus Diamond G range, he was certain of it—and those who stood to gain most by the change in the ownership of the ranch were the three land-hungry neighbors who had continually been the source of trouble.

It was to them he would look first for the killer; a connection with Henry Kanin, Con Mayo, and Gus McNabb, in that order. Chances were a hired killer had been brought in, a man who was a stranger in the valley. Tracking him down was something he would have to do himself. There was no point in just leaving it up to Luke Gable. The lawman was old, past his prime, and worst of all, was under Kanin's thumb. He could, of course, appeal to the sheriff at the county seat, Gable's superior, but that would take time. Besides, a man should draw his own water and not look to others to do it for him.

And find the killer he would. Maybe he and his pa

had not been as close as they should have been, but there was a reason for that—one stemming from the death of his mother at the time of his birth. Regardless of their strained relationship, however, Burl Honeymaker was his father, his only kin, and blood ties counted.

But before he could begin the search he needed to get things in hand at the ranch. An idea he'd long had about unused Diamond G range could now be put into effect. There would be those who might immediately interpret what he intended to do as a confirmation of suspected weakness, but he cared little about what anyone thought.

The important thing was that by so doing he could possibly stop the range war that certainly would break out if any of the ranchers attempted to take by force a part of his land. He would never countenance that; he was willing to follow a plan of aiding his neighbors but there was enough of Burl Honeymaker in his make-up to resist any moves toward taking over his range.

Tom pulled to a halt. The rocky shelves and weedy embankments of the butte area were ahead. He sat for a time studying the ragged formations, thinking back, remembering how on different occasions he'd seen his father sitting his horse on one of the high points, gazing out across the land below. Several times Tom had wondered what he was thinking about in those moments; was he remembering the past, the days gone and how they had been? Was he having regrets? Or was he dreaming of the future, of an even greater Diamond G ranch? They were questions that would now forever go unanswered.

Swinging the sorrel gelding he was riding around to the north end of the bluffs, Tom guided him to the crest and headed out onto the largest of several small plateaus. A welter of hoof prints hammered into the rocky soil bore evidence of the countless times Burl Honeymaker had visited that particular area, and drove home to Tom immediately the conviction that whoever it was that had bushwhacked him had known of his liking for that spot and so had lain in wait for him to come. Logically, the killer was someone familiar with Burl's habits.

Dismounting, Tom fell to examining the ground. He discovered where his father had fallen from the saddle, noted the two grooves made by the heels of his boots when Murcer had dragged the body a short distance to where it could be loaded on the buckskin.

The killer's bullet had ripped into his pa from behind, Tom recalled, and turning, he looked back up the slope to a line of brush and rocks some fifty yards distant. Likely that was where the bushwhacker had hidden. Leaving the sorrel, he climbed to that point. The glint of sunlight upon metal caught his attention, and reaching into a clump of mountain mahogany, he recovered a brass cartridge casing. It was shiny and bright, showed no effects of corrosion that it would had it been there for any length of time. Undoubtedly it had been levered from the rifle that had killed Burl.

Tom examined it thoughtfully. . . . Forty-four caliber . . . common as dirt. Just about every man in the valley would own a weapon of similar bore. It offered no help, but he thrust it into a pocket anyway and continued the search for other items that might prove of value.

He found nothing, not even clear boot prints. The loose gravel was inches deep along the shelf and there were only scuff marks to be seen. Giving up finally, he wheeled, headed back to the sorrel. The only thing he'd learned was that the killer had known of his pa's frequent visits to the ledge, and when he gave that deeper consideration, he realized such meant little; it did not necessarily prove that someone in the Cibola Valley had been the killer; a hired gun brought in to do the job could have been told by the man buying his services of Burl Honeymaker's routine. And if he—

Tom's thoughts came to an abrupt halt. Something plucked at the slack in his shirt. In that same fragment of time the sharp crack of a rifle reached his ears. Reacting instantly, he spun, dived for cover behind a large boulder a stride or so below him. The rifle snapped again. The bullet struck the slanting surface of the rock, shrilled off into space.

Flat on his belly, Tom peered around the end of the boulder. The rifleman was somewhere above and to his right, he judged, figuring the angle. Removing his hat, he pushed it above the top of the boulder. The marksman responded, his bullet again screaming off into the afternoon sunlight as it glanced off the hard surface of the rock.

Tom smiled tautly. That was all he needed—that telltale puff of smoke that marked the bushwhacker's location. Pulling back, he rolled away from the rock, and keeping deep in the brush, worked his way into a wide circle toward the killer.

Fifty yards away from the ledge he came to the end of the ragged, tangled growth and there cut left, began to climb the steep grade toward the embankment. The smoke had come from a position just beyond it. Mid-way he pulled up short. The dry rattle of sliding gravel was a sudden, distinct sound on the warm air.

Cursing, Tom drew his pistol and started up the grade, running as best he could over the loose surface, eyes probing the slope ahead for a glimpse of the killer. Breathless, legs trembling from the exertion, he gained the crest. Sweat pouring off him, he dropped to a crouch. A blur of motion on ahead caught his attention. Instinctively he threw himself to one side as the rifle blasted once more.

He still had no good view of the bushwhacker, but he snapped a shot into the shadows where he had seen movement anyway. Again rocking to the side, he rushed on, pointing for a stand of dense mahogany a short distance to his right. Gaining its shelter, he halted, sucking hard for breath. Almost in that same moment the quick, hard pound of hoofs came to him.

Lunging to his feet, Honeymaker raced into the undergrowth, striving to get a look at the fleeing outlaw. He caught only a glimpse of the horse—a bay with a white-stockinged hind leg—and little else of value. Deep in a maze of ragged brush and scattered rock, he could see only a short distance in any direction. The killer had chosen an ideal spot in which to hide.

Breathing heavily, still trembling from his efforts, Tom listened to the faintly echoing hoofbeats. There was no doubt in his mind the man who had taken shots at him and his father's killer were one and the same. Whoever it was, he was out to finish the job; someone wanted the Honeymaker family wiped out completely.

Holstering his gun, a sullen anger burning within him, Tom doubled back to the waiting sorrel. Mounting, he gave the area a final, sweeping glance and then started down the slope. There was no point in trying to follow the killer; tracking would be an impossibility in such wild, rough country; moreover, the echoes had made it difficult to determine which direction he had taken.

Honeymaker glanced at the scorched hole in his shirt. The bullet hadn't missed by much. An inch or so to the right and he'd be lying back there on the ledge either dead or slowly bleeding to death. From then on, he thought grimly, or at least until he'd made known his plans and put them into operation, it would be wise to move about with care.

A time later, with the sun beginning to drop low in the west, he broke out of the ragged hills onto the flat that led up to the ranch. He slowed the gelding's pace. A half a dozen riders, still in the saddle, were drawn up in front of the house. Facing them were Pearly Quinn, old Manuel the yard hand, and another of the Diamond G riders.

It didn't require a closer look to recognize the man in the center of the visiting party . . . Henry Kanin.

Tom swung wide of the yard, moved unseen to the corner of the house, and there behind a windbreak of tamarisk, sized up the callers, Kanin and four Box K men, one of which was Lou Cobb, his foreman. He couldn't hear what was being said but it was a foregone conclusion that Henry Kanin had not come to extend condolences.

Touching the sorrel lightly with his spurs, Honeymaker continued on to the rear of the house and dismounted at the hitchrack. Entering the low-roofed building by the back door, he made his way through to the front. Then, hand resting lightly on the butt of his pistol, he stepped out onto the porch.

Kanin's head came up sharply and his small eyes hardened. Quinn and the men with him looked around, greeted him expressionlessly.

"You been inside eavesdropping all the time?" the rancher asked icily.

Kanin's towering arrogance rubbed at Tom's nerves. "Maybe," he replied coolly.

"Then there ain't no use of me hashing over what I just told Quinn—"

"Do it anyway."

Kanin stirred angrily. It was evident he expected to find Tom in a more humble state and the younger man's belligerency rankled him.

"Came here to talk—give you a chance to straighten things out."

"Straighten out what things?"

"Turning loose of some of your range. With your pa gone—"

"How'd you know he was dead? Only happened a few hours ago."

Kanin shrugged. "Happens I was in Gable's office when some cowhand of yours come for him."

"And before the dirt's dry on his grave you're here wanting to talk business."

"There'll be others. Been a rule of mine to get there first. You willing to listen?"

"I'll listen—but you'll be wasting your breath. Got plans of my own."

Two more Honeymaker riders drifted up from the bunkhouse: Tularosa, the slim, dark vaquero, and Gabe Archer. They joined with Quinn and the others, forming a line near Tom. Kanin's men merely looked on in silence.

The rancher studied Honeymaker coldly. "If you take my advice, you won't plan nothing—leastwise for a while. Things are going to change around here."

"Any changes being made on the Diamond G will be done by me," Tom said. "If you've got something to say, say it and move on."

Kanin's face was a deep red and his jaw was set. "All right, I'll make no bones about it. I need more range and I need it now—"

"You claimed to be needing it years ago. Telling me that's nothing new."

"Got more stock coming in—new herd. Special stuff I bought over in Texas. I want that place you call the Rinconada to run them on."

30

"Not a chance," Tom said flatly.

He could take this opportunity to tell Kanin what he had in mind to do with some of his range, but the man's attitude irked him. He'd make him wait and hear it with McNabb and Con Mayo.

"I'm willing to buy—ten cents an acre for what's in that canyon and any more you're agreeable to sell. Same offer I tried to make to your pa."

"And my answer's the same as his. None of my land is for sale."

"Good price. Save yourself a lot of trouble if you'll take it."

"Good price!" Pearly Quinn snorted. "Hell, a dime a acre ain't even close to what that Rinconada's worth."

"It's aplenty for grass you ain't using," one of Kanin's rider's observed.

"Worth that much to just let it stand there and grow," the old cook shot back.

"Land ain't worth nothing to a dead man," the Box K rider said dryly.

Tom smiled faintly, nodded to Kanin. "Figured it'd come out sooner or later. With Pa dead you reckoned you could buffalo me into giving in—something you could never make him do. Well, nothing's changed, Kanin. You move one cow over the line onto my range without my say-so and you've got a shooting war on your hands."

The rancher's lips pulled into a hard grin. "Like you've said, Burl Honeymaker's dead—and that makes a hell of a big difference. Might just learn you've bit off more'n you can chew."

"Something you can find out if you're of a mind. I don't want trouble—fact is I'm trying to avoid it, but don't push me. I won't stand for being crowded."

Henry continued to smile in his bland, fixed way. After a time he murmured, "We'll see," and jerking his head at the men beside him, wheeled his horse about and rode out of the yard.

Tom watched in silence until the riders had reached the gate and swung onto the road, and then he turned to face Quinn and the others. Tularosa met his glance with a wry shake of his head.

"I think, *muchacho*, there is much trouble coming now."

"Could be," Honeymaker said quietly, "but they'll be the ones to start it, not me—"

"Then you best grab Bill Jacks and his bunch," Quinn said quickly. "He's getting all set to do some riding."

Tom shifted his attention to the bunkhouse. "Where is he?"

"Ain't got no idea, but I reckon he'll be showing up for supper pretty soon. Heard him telling Ed Davis to be ready to go after they got done eating."

"They won't be going anywhere," Honeymaker said. "Aim to hold a meeting right about then, explain what I'm going to do. Want everybody there—especially the old hands. If there's any of them out with the herd, spell them off with some of the new help."

"You ain't figuring on selling out or doing—"

Tom shook his head. "Nothing like that," he replied, and paused as Gabe Archer reached out an arm and pointed at the bullet hole in his shirt.

"When'd you get that?" the old puncher asked, eyes narrowing.

"Couple hours ago when I was up at the buttes."

The men stared at him. "You saying somebody took a shot at you?" Quinn demanded.

32

Honeymaker nodded. "Expect it was the same jasper that put a bullet in Pa. Got away before I could get a look at him."

Tularosa muttered something in Spanish. Archer hawked, spat. "Maybe I got a plumb good hunch who that might've been—"

"Who?"

"Joe Kanin."

Tom frowned. "What makes you think it was him?"

"Always with his pa when there's something going on like coming here. Learning how to be a big rancher, I guess. Well, this time he wasn't along."

"By hell, that's the truth!" Quinn declared. "And I wouldn't put it past him being the one. Could've done it on his own, sort of to help out his pa—or old Henry just maybe put him up to it."

Joe Kanin . . . Tom gave the possibility thought. It could very well have been him; he might have taken it upon himself to bring Box K's range problems to a head, or as Pearly Quinn suggested, acted on his father's instructions—and the fact that he was not accompanying Henry Kanin and the other riders was unusual. But there was nothing beyond that to go on—no solid proof of any kind; and there were plenty more in the Cibola Valley with the same problem who could have decided to settle things with a bullet.

"For my money he's the goddam bushwhacker that done it," Quinn said firmly, "and I'm ready to—"

"Still need some proof," Tom broke in. "Can't just jump at a thing like that."

"Then I reckon we best start working to get proof—"

"My job. You've got your own chores to do—and if

things go the way I'm planning we'll all be plenty busy around here from tomorrow on."

"What about the deputy? You going to say something to him?"

"I'll handle it myself," Honeymaker replied, and hesitated as the slice of iron-tired wheels cutting into the sandy soil and the thud of a horse's hoofs came to him. Turning, he glanced toward the gate. A buggy drawn by a thick-bodied gray was moving up the drive.

"It's Gus McNabb's womenfolks," Archer said. "Heard about your pa and wanting to say their sorrys, I expect."

Pearly Quinn grunted skeptically. "More'n likely old Gus sent them. Figures if he can't get next to you one way, he maybe can another. . . . Reckon I'd best get back to my kitchen."

6

Tom heard Quinn turn away, nodded absently to the vague excuses uttered by Archer and the other two men as they followed the cook's example and moved off, leaving him to greet his visitors alone.

There was likely much truth in Pearly Quinn's assessment of the situation. He scarcely knew Mrs. McNabb and while the girl, Ellie, and he had attended school in Rimrock together when they were kids, and later he had danced with her on occasion at the church sociables before the Honeymaker presence at such became unwelcome and he had stopped going, she was equally a stranger.

Waiting until the buggy had rolled up to him and halted, he touched the brim of his hat and stepped up to the vehicle.

"Good evening, ladies."

Mrs. McNabb, a heavily built, healthy looking woman with red cheeks, turned sideways on the seat to dismount. Taking her by the arm, Honeymaker assisted her from the buggy.

"We're very sorry about your pa," she said.

"Thank you," Tom murmured, and reached up to aid Ellie.

The girl had changed considerably, he noted as he took her elbow. She had slimmed down, was fixing her dark hair differently, and her eyes seemed larger. Too, she was much prettier than he remembered.

"How are you, Tom?" she asked in a quiet voice, and then smiled ruefully. "That wasn't a very smart thing to say at a time like this, was it?"

He shrugged, pulled back as the girl leaned forward and procured a plate covered with a square of white cloth from the bed of the buggy.

"We know you have a cook," Mrs. McNabb said, "but we wanted to bring something. . . . It's a fresh apple pie."

"Obliged to you—it'll be a real treat. Pearly's not too good on fancy things like pies," he said, taking the plate from the girl. Nodding toward the porch, he added: "You can sit there if you like. You'll find it comfortable."

Standing aside, he waited until the women had seated themselves, and then crossing behind them, he opened the door leading into a room that ordinarily would be a parlor but instead had served as a sort of office for his father. Depositing the dish on a nearby table, he returned to the porch.

"Sorry I don't have anything to offer you. Company's something we don't get much. I can bring you some coffee."

"No, thank you," Mrs. McNabb said at once.

He glanced questioningly at Ellie. She smiled, shook her head. "We can only stay a minute—"

"But we wanted to drop by," the older woman finished. "It was a terrible thing to happen. Terrible."

Tom, leaning against one of the roof supports, nodded for lack of any better reply. A rattle of pans was coming from the cookshack where Quinn was busy at preparing the evening meal, and the reedy music of a harmonica being played by someone in the bunkhouse hung faintly in the evening air.

"I suppose you've already held the services," Mrs. McNabb said after a slight pause.

"This morning—late. Was no use waiting."

"We would've come if we'd known."

Tom felt Ellie's eyes upon him. He glanced at her, and she looked away.

"We never see you at church any more," Mrs. McNabb said.

"No, we sort of lost out—"

The older woman bobbed vigorously. "It's a shame, a terrible shame, the way things've turned out around here."

Here it comes, Tom thought. *She'll be inviting me over for supper next. Gus has told her exactly what to say and what not to mention.*

But it was Ellie who spoke next. "We used to have good times at those sociables. I'm sorry it all ended."

"Don't they hold them any more?"

"No, it got so no one came—that is, not enough people to make it worthwhile, anyway—so the parson just stopped having them. Actually, only a few people go to church now days."

"Maybe it'll all change," Tom commented, the thought coming to him that such could be a possibility once the plan he had for lessening tension in the valley was put into effect.

"I hope so," the girl said, fingering her lace-edged handkerchief. "There's so little else to do, besides work, I mean. . . . I guess we'd better go, Mama. Tom has things to do, I'm sure."

Honeymaker drew himself upright as the women got to

37

their feet. Somewhere beyond the corrals a dove cooed, the sound lonely and forlorn in the fading daylight.

"Those birds always seem so mournful," Mrs. McNabb murmured, moving across the porch.

Tom helped her back into the buggy, pivoted and assisted Ellie onto the seat. "I'm obliged to you for coming—and for the pie."

"You're welcome. Want to say how sorry I am about your pa, too."

"Appreciate that because I know very few people feel that way. But that's the way it is. I'll return your plate first chance I get."

"There's no hurry."

She was looking directly at him, her eyes blue and utterly frank, and Tom was again aware of how much she had changed and of the woman she had become. If Gus McNabb had trumped up the visit as a means for softening the bad feeling between the two ranches, he was certain Ellie had no hand in it.

"It be all right if I ride by sometime to see you—just talk?" he asked, hesitantly.

Ellie smiled, gathered up the lines. "I'd like that, Tom . . . good-by," she said, and slapping the old work mare smartly with the slack in the leathers, cut the buggy about and drove toward the gate.

7

Tom Honeymaker halted just outside the door of the kitchen-shack, as the rambling structure housing both the cooking and dining facilities of the Diamond G was called. Beyond it he could hear the usual rumble of talk, the clatter of knives and forks against pans and crockery that accompanied meals served on the log table at which the crew faced each other from either side.

Except for a half a dozen of the newer men delegated to night-watch the herd, the entire crew would be present and this was to be the first time since the death of his father he would face the majority of them. Taking a deep breath, he laid his hand on the latch, opened the thick, pegged-timber panel, and stepped inside. Immediately the confusion of sound slackened, and then died off into a tight hush.

Tom stood motionless just within the entrance, letting his eyes sweep over the men. They had ceased eating, were turned to him, some with a secret sort of expectation showing on their features, others merely watching. In that next breath of time understanding came to him. Bill Jacks was in the chair at the head of the table—a place ordinarily occupied by Burl Honeymaker when he chose to eat with his crew.

The men were awaiting his reaction, speculating no doubt as to how he would meet the affront. Personally he could care less about sitting in the place reserved for his father, but he realized that it was expected of him, and if he permitted the burly foreman to usurp what they considered the symbol of authority, their estimation of him would suffer . . . and with what lay ahead he needed their support.

Nodding to all in general, he crossed to where Jacks sat, took hold of the top crosspiece of the chair's back.

"You're in the wrong place, Bill," he said in a firm voice.

The foreman twisted about, looked up insolently. He had a hard, square face, red hair that was matched in color by a stubble of beard and a thick mustache. A surly sort of man, he was a decade or so older than Tom and never a friend.

"That right?" he drawled.

Honeymaker said, "Move, unless you want to eat your grub on the floor," and tipped the chair forward.

Jacks frantically grabbed for the edge of the table to maintain balance. Someone farther down laughed. Anger flushed the foreman's features, and then abruptly he brought a forced smile to his lips.

"Why, sure, Mister Boss-man," he said, gathering up his plate and coffee mug. "Reckon I just wasn't thinking."

Rising, covering his retreat with a laugh, he stepped away from the end of the table, swaggered to a vacant chair at the end of the row.

"Wasn't aiming to tromp on your toes, Junior," Jacks said, still struggling to save face. "I'm sorry as all get out."

Tom made no reply. Motioning to the young Mexican boy who served as Pearly Quinn's helper to bring him a plate and other necessary items, he sat down. The crew resumed their eating, some with quiet smiles, others—those who hung around Bill Jacks—with no show of expression on their faces. There was little talk thereafter, and when the meal was over, Tom got to his feet.

"Called you all here at one time to get a few things said," he began, glancing along the table.

To his left were Gabe Archer, Tularosa, Jim Heston, Manuel, and Lafe Diebold. All were old hands on the Diamond G. Opposite them and down the right flank of the table he noted Ed Davis, Charley Murcer, Pete Carver, Ernie Tolliver, and last in the line the man they ran with, Jacks. Quinn, arms folded across his chest, soiled white apron tucked to one side, leaned against the doorway leading into the adjoining kitchen.

"When we going after the bastard that shot down your pa?" Bill Jacks called, tipping his chair to its back legs. "Appears to me—"

"You're not," Tom replied flatly. "That's a job the deputy and I will take care of. All of you're going to be busy working cattle. Starting in the morning we'll—"

"You're making a mistake," Jacks continued. "If we don't do something about your pa's killing, Kanin and Mayo and some of them others'll get the wrong idea, and first thing you know they'll be swarming in on us like buzzards after a dead cow."

"That's for dang sure!" Ed Davis declared.

"What we've got to do first off is take a ride over to Kanin's place, set a couple of fires, maybe stampede some of his herd, things like that. Then we go to Con Mayo's and the Scotchman's, give them a taste of the same. Got to let them know that nothing's changed around here—and we best do it tonight."

A chorus of agreement came up from the foreman's side of the table. Honeymaker shook his head.

"No. We're finished with that kind of thing."

"Finished?" Jacks shouted. "What the hell you mean by that?"

"Just what it sounds like. I'm putting a stop to this night-riding and all the hoorawing that's been going on. I'm figuring to—"

"See!" Davis yelled, coming half out of his chair and leveling a finger at Jacks. "It's just like I told you! He ain't got the guts to—"

Tularosa was suddenly on his feet. His dark features were quiet but threat lay in his eyes. "You will sit, my friend, and say nothing," he murmured, casually dropping a hand to the knife hanging from his belt.

Davis threw an angry look at the vaquero and settled back. The Mexican resumed his seat.

"I'm aiming to bring a little peace to this country," Tom continued. "There's been more than enough trouble—most of it caused by Diamond G. Tomorrow I'm going to start changing that. I'm turning loose of all my range east and south of Coyote Arroyo, handing it over to Kanin, McNabb, and Mayo."

"No!" Bill Jacks blurted in a strangled voice. "That's more'n thirty thousand acres—all good grass!"

"And land we've never used," Honeymaker said evenly. "All of them need more grazing. That's been the cause of the trouble around here—my pa hanging onto range he didn't have use for and being too bullheaded to give it up."

"Expect he's turning over in his grave right now hearing you say that—"

"Let him. He was a proud man. Never could back off no

matter what. I look at things differently. We've still got more than enough grass, and I'm willing to live and let live."

Tom paused, glanced around the table. There was little he could read on the stolid faces of the older crew members, but Jacks's friends, taking their cue from the foreman, were showing their disapproval.

"I'll be sending word to Kanin and the others telling them to meet me at the line shack down there at noon tomorrow. Be giving them the word then. Meanwhile, in the morning early I want all hands to start drifting the herd north—to the Rinconada. Want the stock to graze in there for the rest of the summer. That'll give the rest of the range a chance to come back before it gets cold."

"I ain't going to let you do it," Bill Jacks said slowly, wagging his head. "I figure I owe your pa and best way I can pay him back is to not let you pull a damn fool stunt like you're talking about. We ain't giving up no range and we're going to keep on saving the Rinconada just like he'd want."

"He's dead, and you've got nothing to say about it," Tom snapped. "Better get that squared around inside your head. I'm doing what I figure ought to've been done a long time ago and if it's not to your liking you can either swallow it anyway, or move on."

"You're getting mighty highhanded now that old Burl ain't around to call you down," the redhead drawled. "How long you think you can keep this ranch running going soft like you are, and giving it away?"

"I'll be here this time next year and for plenty of years after that," Honeymaker replied. "Now, do you all understand what I want done?"

Archer and the riders flanking him nodded. There was no response from Davis and the men seated on the foreman's side of the table. All appeared to be awaiting word from the redhead.

The quiet ran on for a time and then Jacks let his chair come forward with a thump. "Yeh, reckon we do. . . . You all done yammering?"

"Done—except for one thing. Nobody leaves the ranch tonight. Means everybody. Can't take a chance on there being any trouble. Understand?"

"Sure do," Jacks said, smirking. "Me'n the boys'll just set down and play us a few hands of poker, then turn in like good little fellows. That what you want?"

"That's what I want," Tom said.

Sitting at the table an hour or so later with Archer, Tularosa, and Pearly Quinn, cups of black coffee and a wedge of Mrs. McNabb's apple pie in front of each, Tom considered their dissatisfied expressions.

"I take it you don't go for what I'm doing."

Quinn laid down his fork, brushed at his mouth. "I'm thinking it's a fine thing, but I just ain't sure how it'll strike Con Mayo and the others."

Gabe Archer nodded slowly. "Same thing's digging at my mind. Could give them the idea maybe they could waltz right in any time they took the notion, cut themselves out another chunk of the Diamond G."

"You figure I'm soft like Bill Jacks said?"

"Nope, sure don't. I think you're doing what you believe's right—but the Lord only knows how Mayo and Henry Kanin will look at it . . . and Gus McNabb."

"The handout ends with the land below the arroyo. Anybody tries helping himself to more will have a fight on his hands," Honeymaker said quietly, and turned to the vaquero.

"Anything you want to say, *amigo?* Like to know how the three of you feel. Rest don't matter."

Tularosa's shoulders stirred. "What you will do, *muchacho*, is a good thing, but I have worry for Bill Jacks. He will give you much trouble before this is done. It would have been better to rid yourself of him and those *culebras* who suckle with him."

"Need all of them. Short of help now. Anyway, I think he savvys where he stands around here. If he gets out of line once more, he's fired, however."

A silence followed, broken finally by Pearly Quinn.

"That was mighty good pie," he observed, absently.

Archer added his favorable comment. The vaquero nodded. Tom drank the last of the coffee in his mug, set the thick container back on the table.

"Like to know for sure you're with me—"

"Hell, you ought to know better'n ask us that," Quinn said at once. "Maybe we ain't so sure how it'll all turn out, but you're the boss and that's good enough for me—for us all, I reckon. We'll be standing by you same as we did your pa—right or wrong."

"Can't ask for more than that," Honeymaker said, "and I'm obliged to you. . . . Might as well finish the last of this pie."

8

Shortly after daybreak, with the morning meal finished, Tom gathered the crew in front of the bunkhouse. The night's chill still hung in the air and the men, shuffling about restlessly, were edgy and uncommunicative.

"You know what's to be done," he said. "Move the herd up into the Rinconada. Expect it'll take a couple of days, maybe longer. Some of the stock's drifted pretty far west and you'll have to swing wide to get them. Same thing'll hold true for the east range. . . . If you have any problems Jacks will be around somewhere."

"No, reckon he won't," the redhead said in his slow, drawling way. "I'm quitting."

Tom looked more closely at the rider. Apparently there had been quite a bit of drinking along with the card playing Bill and his friends had engaged in during the night.

"Means you're leaving me without a foreman."

"Well, smart as you are that ain't likely to be no big sweat."

Honeymaker held on to his rising temper. "Mind telling me why you're pulling out?"

"Hell, no. I plain ain't about to work for some gutless outfit like this'n's turned into. Goes for my pals here, too." Jacks ducked his head at the men grouped around him—Davis, Charley Murcer, Tolliver, and Pete Carver.

Tom faced them. "That the way it is? You quitting?"

Davis nodded. "Sure are—every one of us. And we're wanting our time—"

"You'll get it," Tom snapped brusquely, and swung back to the remaining members of the crew. "Starting now Gabe Archer's your foreman. Take your orders from him. Any questions?"

Jim Heston pulled off his hat, scrubbed at the back of his neck. "Ain't going to be but four, maybe five of us working the herd. Don't hardly see how we can get much done."

"I'll hire on more help soon as I can ride into town. Just get started and be doing the best you can."

"Me and Manuel'll give you a hand quick's we get our chores wound up," Quinn said, coming up from the kitchen. "One of you saddle us couple of them broomtails, have them ready for us. We'll catch up."

The riders began to move off, heading for the corrals where they would rope out a horse for the day. Tom, motioning to Bill Jacks and his followers, turned back to the ranch house, and taking the necessary cash from the tin box kept in his father's desk, paid them off. As they wheeled to go, the redhead looked back over his shoulder.

"Reckon you're one of them kind that has to learn the hard way," he said with a wide grin. "Well, you're sure going to be doing just that. . . . So long, kid."

Still clinging to his temper, Tom made no reply, simply stepped back into the house and closed the door. There was nothing to be gained by giving in to anger and taking on Bill Jacks with his fists. Before it was over he'd likely have Ed Davis and the others on his hands; but the day would come, if Jacks continued to stay in the Cibola Valley, when he'd find the opportunity to settle a few old scores with him.

The night-hawkers came in, and meeting them in the cookshack, he called for three volunteers to carry his summons to the ranchers. It had been an easy shift for the riders, the herd having given them no trouble, and all six of the men made known their willingness.

Honeymaker chose the ones he felt most suited to perform the chore and then announced the change in foreman. There was a general nod of approval to that, with Irby Lewis, one of the older hands, expressing his feelings about it vocally.

"Can't nobody do a job for a man and be out helling around every blasted night, like him and them other's've been doing."

Tom came to attention. "That include last night?"

"Sure does. I seen them go riding by—was about ten, maybe eleven o'clock. Heading south. For town, I reckon."

"They come in just before first light," another of the punchers volunteered. "Was circling the herd when I seen them. They didn't spot me."

"Me neither," Lewis said.

Honeymaker shrugged. He should have expected it from Jacks and his crowd; under no circumstances would they take any orders from him—but he was through with them now and he need waste no more thought on them. He could only hope they caused no trouble in Rimrock that would endanger his plans for restoring the Diamond G to the good graces of the townspeople.

"Any of the rest of you feel like working extra, I can use some help on the drive," he said then. "Mean a little more money to you. Just report to Gabe Archer. He'll tell you what to do."

Quinn, bringing a cup of coffee to Tom, listened to the

comments of the men, all of whom were stating their desire to accept the offer, in silence. When it was settled, he jerked a thumb at the men delegated to carry the word to Kanin and the other ranchers.

"Could let just one of them do that. It'd mean Gabe'd have a couple more to help out."

"Thought of doing that but then I figured I'd best send word to each one. Feeling between them's not much better than they have for us and it'd be like Mayo to get riled up if he thought Kanin or Gus McNabb got sent for first and was being favored. Same goes for Henry."

"Yeh, expect that's right. They're all touchier'n old she-bear with a couple of cubs. . . . You leaving now?"

Tom nodded. "Aim to follow along the east line, do what I can to get the strays pointed north while I work toward Coyote Arroyo. Want to get there on time."

"You meeting them by yourself?"

"Sure. Why not?"

"Nothing special, but you sort of keep your eyes peeled. I don't trust them jaspers any farther'n I could throw the barn, considering how they felt about your pa. Goes twice't for Con Mayo. He had a mighty big hate on for Burl. Like as not he's feeling the same towards you."

"Once they hear what I've got to say things ought to ease off. . . . So long."

Tom rode out a few minutes later, angling toward the southeastern edge of his range, astride a long-legged black the horse wrangler had cut out for him. It was a fine, pleasant morning, warm now with the sun climbing steadily into a steely, cloudless sky.

Field larks were exploding from the grass at the passage of the black, soaring off into the clean, dry air, and overhead a flock of crows were straggling irregularly for the hills to the west where they would remain until nightfall.

He hoped his offer would be well received by Kanin and the ranchers, and the peace the valley had never really known come to be. It was a fine place to live and he could think of nothing better or more to his liking than spending the rest of his days on the Diamond G raising cattle, perhaps going into the breeding of fine horses, while at the same time, with the ill-feeling his father had created finally washed away, becoming a well thought of member of the community.

And there was Ellie McNabb. He was finding himself impatient to see her again and get better acquainted. That shouldn't be too hard, he reasoned, once he'd made amends to her father. It was nice to think of her being a part of his future.

A small jag of steers appeared off in a cluster of cedars to his left. He swung the black in behind, hazed them out of the scrub trees, and started them moving northward. One of the riders would pick them up once they were beyond the rise now lifting up before them and were in the long swale that flowed out from its farther side, and keep them drifting on to join with the main herd.

He rode on, thoughts vagrant at times, deep with plans in other moments. . . . As soon as he had squared away with the ranchers, he'd ride into town, try to find hands to replace Jacks and the others who'd quit. He didn't hold out much hope for finding punchers in Rimrock who were looking for work, and it just could be that he'd be forced to go on to Eagle Rock, the next town. It was a half a day's journey on to the east.

Another scatter of strays drew his attention an hour or so

later and he spent considerable time getting them together
and moving into the right direction. After that he glanced
at the sun, saw that it was drawing near mid-day, and
bringing the black about, spurred him into a fast lope for
the line shack at Coyote Arroyo.

It was shortly after noon when he reached the weathered
old log structure, once the home of a prospector who had
sought gold in the stream that in those days coursed down
the deep wash. His hopes had died and he had eventually
moved on, leaving the cabin to be made use of by Burl
Honeymaker when he gathered in the land that became the
vast Diamond G.

There was no sign of the ranchers, and Tom, pulling to
a halt on the shaded side of the shack, dismounted and settled down to wait. The minutes dragged by. A half hour
passed. An hour. Worry began to tag at his mind. Had
something gone wrong? Had his riders failed to deliver the
messages for some reason? Or were Kanin and the others
simply refusing to meet with him, electing to have nothing
to do with a Honeymaker? Basing their thoughts on past
experience, they could be fearing a trick and—

A roll of dust began to show in the south. Tom smiled
in relief. They were coming. It seemed a large party judg-
ing from the tan and gray cloud, but he reckoned there
could be more in it than just Kanin, Mayo, and McNabb.
Very possibly it also included owners of some of the smaller
outfits on below the Box K brought in on the meeting.

The riders emerged slowly from the distant haze, became more distinct. Kanin, his son Joe; Con Mayo, Gus
McNabb, and one of his hired hands—and the three punchers he'd dispatched to summon them. Tom frowned. He
had expected his men to return to the ranch as soon as they

had completed their missions and assist Archer and the others in moving the herd; had they been compelled to stay and accompany the ranchers to the line shack? If so, why?

A mixture of anger and uneasiness stirred through Tom. Hitching at his gun belt, he moved away from the side of the cabin, walked forward until he was at the edge of a small meadow across which the riders would be coming. Squinting into the glare, he studied the men.

Kanin was in the center of the group, with Joe at his right flank. The face of the older man was dark, grim. Mayo, on his left, was evidently in a like frame of mind. Gus McNabb, a few paces to the rear with the three Diamond G cowhands and the one he'd brought from his own spread, as usual betrayed no emotion on his ruddy features.

They reached the meadow, traversed it, walking their horses slowly, and drew to a halt half a dozen strides away. At that moment Tom heard sound behind him, threw a quick glance over his shoulder. Tularosa, a rifle cradled in his arms, was leaning against the corner of the old shack, big hat tipped forward over his eyes.

"What the hell—"

The vaquero made a slight motion with a hand. "It is not wise to walk among wolves alone, *muchacho*," he said languidly.

"Honeymaker!"

At Kanin's sharp voice Tom came back around, the very timbre of the man's imperious tones raising the hackles on his neck. No matter the outcome of matters in the valley Henry Kanin was someone he'd never find a liking for and call a friend.

"What's this all about? You up to some kind of a trick that'll—"

"No trick," Tom replied evenly, and beckoned to his riders, "Come over here."

The three men hesitated briefly, glancing aside at Kanin and Mayo, and then rode forward, swung in beside the line shack, and stopped.

"Speak up!" Con Mayo said in a tight voice. "It wouldn't take much for me to throw down on you, settle up right now for what—"

"No, *señor*," Tularosa warned softly, drawing himself upright. "You will not do that unless you have a wish to die."

The rancher swore, stared hard at the vaquero, and spat. "Might've knowed . . . expect you've got some more like him stashed around handy."

"No, and he came on his own. What I intend to say calls for nobody standing by me with a gun."

"Then say it—"

"I'm pulling out of this end of my range, turning it over to you three to be divided among you. Means everything south and east of—"

"The hell you say!" Kanin shouted, his face going a bright red. "After what your bunch done to us last night— you're pulling out of the valley complete—and for good! We're taking over all of your range."

9

Honeymaker stiffened. "Don't know what you're talking about."

"Don't give us that bull!" Mayo shot back. "That bunch you sent was seen—recognized."

Abruptly a tenseness was filling the air. Tom looked from one to the other of the ranchers. "Still don't know anything about—"

"Bill Jacks works for you, don't he? And Ed Davis and Charley Murcer—and them other two—"

"Ernie Tolliver and Pete Carver," the younger Kanin supplied.

"Yeh, that's them. . . . They're all working for you, ain't they?"

"They did. Quit this morning."

Henry Kanin laughed scornfully. "Oh, sure! Anyways, we're talking about last night. They rode into my place, set fire to the feed barn and a wagon shed. Shot one of my yard hands when he tried to stop them."

"Hit me next," Con Mayo said. "Killed three horses I had in a back corral. Just done it for no other reason than pure, goddam meanness! Cut loose then on the house, put bullets through all the window glass. When they was riding out one of them hollered, 'That's for old Burl!' You still claiming you don't know nothing about it?"

Tom shook his head. It was clear now where Jacks and his friends had gone during the night and what they had done; it was equally apparent their actions had been to spite him and not because they felt a need to exact a measure of vengeance for Burl Honeymaker's murder. He shifted his glance to Gus McNabb. The old Scotsman stirred uneasily.

"The same, somewhat. Rode into my place, emptied their guns into a little bunch of cows I had penned up to sell George Slater. Killed five of them, maybe'll lose a couple more."

"Sorry about all that," Tom said, "but like I've—"

"Sorry—good God! That's a fine thing to be telling us!" Kanin shouted, his mouth working with anger. "Well, mister, it ends right here! We've put up with that kind of doings from your pa for thirty years—and we're calling a halt. We're not letting you carry on in the same go-to-hell way—"

"Saying it again," Tom cut in sharply. "I didn't have anything to do with what happened to any of you last night. I gave strict orders that nobody was to leave the ranch. Jacks and the men you saw riding with him went anyway. Whatever they did, they did on their own and I won't be responsible."

"The hell you won't!" Mayo snarled. "They was working for you, and it ain't doing you no good to deny it. And I'm betting they're like as not setting off there in the brush somewheres waiting for you to hail them in if there's need. You're just as full of lousy, two-bit tricks as your pa!"

Honeymaker folded his arms across his chest, fought to keep his voice level. "That's in the past—what my pa did. I'm hoping to wipe the slate clean, start over."

"You think you can make us swallow that? Won't surprise me none to find out you calling us here was only a way to get us off our places so's your bunch could cripple us up some more!"

"No, reason I got you together was to say I realize you're all needing more range and tell you—"

"What you'd be telling us wouldn't be worth no more'n the promises your pa made."

Tom was fast losing control of his anger. He knew he could not blame them too much for the way they felt; his pa had dealt harshly with them, given them nothing but grief, and the activities of Bill Jacks and his crowd that previous night—supposedly all in the name of the Honeymakers—was lending no credence to his sincerity.

"I'll not say this again," he said, his voice low and stiff. "I had nothing to do with last night. You can suit yourself about believing that—and I don't particularly give a damn whether you do or not. Reason you're here is because I wanted to try and make amends for the things my pa might have done to you."

"Yeh, we've heard that from them cowhands you sent to bring us," Kanin said. "You're real willing to hand over all the land on the other side of the wash to us. Now, that's mighty big of you—but we ain't falling for it. First off, it'd be some trick. No Honeymaker ever give away nothing."

"That's for damn sure," Mayo declared.

"No trick. It's land I'm not using and can get along without."

"You're going to be getting along without any of it!" Con Mayo shouted, shaking his fist. "You hear that? We've took all we're going to from you Honeymakers. We're plumb fed up. Ain't nothing ever come out of that goddam Diamond G but trouble, and we're putting a stop to it!"

A stillness settled through Tom. "Meaning?"

"Meaning just this," Henry Kanin said bluntly. "We're running you out of the valley—taking over your place, land, buildings, and cattle. You'll find a draft waiting at the bank covering what we figure it's worth."

Honeymaker listened in icy silence. Within him, however, a full-blown rage had finally reached its peak and was clamoring for release. But only the cords in his neck and the planes of his face betrayed the fact.

"I'll see you all in hell first," he said, spacing the words slowly, distinctly.

"You got twenty-four hours to load up whatever you want and clear out, then we'll be moving in," Mayo said.

"When you do, come with plenty of guns. I've made my try at getting along with you, but you won't have it. All right, that's how it'll be from here on. . . . And another thing while we're all together—one of you murdered my pa, or had it done. And you took a shot at me. Got my ideas who it is and as soon as I'm sure I'll be looking you up."

"You won't be around," Henry Kanin said curtly. "If you're smart you'll be gone—otherwise you'll be dead."

"Don't bet on either one," Tom replied in a brittle voice. "Now, get the hell off my land and don't ever set foot on it again."

The ranchers were unmoving for a long breath, and then one by one they wheeled about, doubled back over the trail they had made coming in. When they were beyond the meadow, Tom turned, walked slowly to where Tularosa and the other Diamond G riders, still in their saddles, were waiting. As he drew near, the vaquero grinned broadly.

"It was spoken well, *muchacho*. I think maybe you are very much like the *patrón*."

"That damned Jacks," Honeymaker muttered, simmering with anger. "Was him that brought this on. Like as not I could have got them to see things my way if he and that bunch of his hadn't pulled the stunt they did."

"Perhaps," Tularosa said, his dark face now sober, "but of that I would not be so sure. Con Mayo has a very large hate, and this Kanin, he is much the same. I think they wish to do this anyway. Those *bribonazos* have just give them the excuse to do so now. They believe that with your *papa* dead it will be a thing of ease to take from you what they could not have when he was living."

"And they're meaning it," one of the riders said, leaning forward and resting a forearm on the horn of his saddle. "Me and Bud and Otto here, we heard them talking. They aim to bring a regular army in here, plain drive you off if you don't pack up and go."

"That'll be the last thing I'll do," Tom said, bringing his attention back to Tularosa. "I want you to ride to the ranch. Tell Pearly Quinn and Gabe Archer what happened and say I said to do everything they can to get the herd moved. I've got to have every cow I own inside the Rinconada by tomorrow noon."

The vaquero, his dark face shining with sweat, nodded. "*Sí, patrón*. Where do you go?"

"Town. Need to hire on some help."

"Have a care—"

"Aim to."

59

"Hate to say this, Mr. Honeymaker," the oldest of the riders said as Tom started toward the black, "but you best not figure on us. Way we see it you ain't got a Chinaman's chance of stopping that bunch when they move in. They was really making big plans."

"Quinn will give you your time when you get to the ranch," Tom snapped impatiently, as he swung onto his horse. "Tell him to pay off anybody else that feels the same as they do," he added to the vaquero. "See you about dark."

10

The hostility in the air was almost tangible. Tom was conscious of it the moment he swung onto Rimrock's main street and pointed the black toward Justin's general store. Jaw set, he kept his eyes straight ahead. It hadn't taken long for news of Bill Jacks's activities to spread, and as was to be expected, the townspeople and all others in the valley were giving credit for the incident to the Diamond G—to him in fact now that Burl Honeymaker was dead.

The confrontation had changed Tom's thinking where others were concerned considerably, and some of the contempt and disdain for people that had typified his father was now beginning to show in him. Ramrod straight, he dismounted, stepped up onto Justin's porch. There, shoulders squared against the driving sunlight, he swept the street with a deliberate, scornful glance.

He was a Honeymaker—the son of old Burl. Like Kanin and Mayo and McNabb, they'd believe nothing he told them; they would believe what they wanted to regardless of the truth. So be it. Lips curled, he moved on across the broad landing, and pulling back the dust-clogged screen door, entered.

Justin, wearing black cotton sleeve guards and a denim bib apron over his work clothes, was behind a counter at the back of the room. Expressionless, he waited until Tom drew to a halt in front of him. Then:

"Something I can do for you?"

Tom's anger, not fully subsided, and barely below the surface, stirred quickly. Here was change. In the past the storekeeper had always maintained a neutral stance. It would seem that now, with Burl out of the picture, he was having second thoughts.

"Can see you've heard," Honeymaker said coldly.

"Know what happened last night, if that's what you mean—and what Henry Kanin and his friends aim to do about it."

"That all?"

"What else is there?"

Tom shrugged, perversity having its way with him. Emory Justin had made up his mind, and attempting to alter it by explanations was not worth the effort.

"Need some cartridges. Half a dozen boxes of forty-fives, a couple of boxes of forty-four forties."

The merchant turned to a shelf behind him, procured the ammunition, and set it on the counter.

"Anything else?"

"That's it."

Wordless, Justin reached under the counter for a flour sack. Holding it open, he placed the boxes inside, gathered a neck, and tied a string about it. Shoving it toward Tom, he crossed his arms, leaned back against the shelving.

"Reckon you know this is going to bust this country wide open," he said.

Honeymaker slung the sack across a shoulder. "You expect me to just back off, let them take over my place?"

"No, of course not."

"Then I've got no choice."

The merchant wagged his head. "There's no cleaning up bad blood, seems."

"And nobody ever forgets, either."

"After the way your pa rode roughshod over folks in this valley, you think they could? He's had people by the throat around here for a lot of years—especially Henry Kanin and Con Mayo. They ain't apt to ever forget."

"Maybe not, but you can't lay it all on Pa. There's plenty of what happened around here that pushed him into taking a stand. I'm not saying he wasn't wrong sometimes, but he was right pretty often, too. I'm finding out how that works myself."

"You might try talking to them. Not saying it'll do any good—not after last night, but for the sake of the country a man ought to keep a range war from breaking out."

"More to it than that. My whole spread's at stake along with my right to live the kind of a life I want. If there's to be any talking done to them somebody else will have to do it now. . . . You getting anxious about my bill—afraid maybe I might not be around to pay it?"

"I'm not worrying—" Justin began, and then paused, glanced toward the door. "Howdy, Luke."

Tom came about, nodded coolly to the lawman. Gable, face stern, moved in nearer, eyes on the sack Honeymaker was carrying. The corners of the small boxes showed plainly through the thin cloth.

"Them's cartridges you're buying," the deputy said, making it an accusation rather than a question.

"Could be," Tom replied laconically.

The deputy bristled. "Well, I'm telling you right now if you're figuring to start trouble—forget it. I won't stand for no—"

"You're talking to the wrong man, Sheriff."

"I'm talking to you!" Gable snapped. "You're the cause of this and I'm ordering you to put a stop to it before it gets going."

"Man's got a right to protect his property. That's what I'll be doing."

Obstinacy was again ruling Tom. It was evident that neither of the men had heard yet of his meeting with the ranchers earlier that day and of his offer to turn over a large slice of Diamond G range to them. Nor had they bothered to get particulars from him, hear his side of the story, relative to the raid Bill Jacks and his hard-case followers had made. Both were assuming him to be guilty of fostering the incident simply because he was Burl Honeymaker's son.

Gable's features were taut. "I'm warning you—"

"Kanin—Mayo—McNabb. They're the ones you need to be shaking your finger at. There'll be no trouble long as they stay off my land. They don't, there'll be some killing. It's that simple. . . . Now, I've got a question for you, Deputy. What've you done about running down my pa's murderer?"

Gable frowned, cleared his throat. "Nothing—yet. Ain't had time. Only happened yesterday."

"If it'd been Henry Kanin would it be taking this long?"

The lawman flushed. "Now, wait a goddam minute—"

"Trail gets colder by the hour," Tom said, moving toward the door. "And the way it looks it's going to be up to me to find him."

"My job, I'll do it," Gable said, regaining his composure. "Where you headed now?"

Honeymaker paused in the doorway. "Don't know as it's any of your business but I'm going over to Sudreth's saloon, see if I can hire on some help. I'm about a half a dozen hands short."

11

Still simmering, Tom Honeymaker stepped out into the open and walked stiffly to his horse. He meant every word he'd said to Luke Gable concerning the lawman's failure to start a search for his father's killer, and there was no doubt in his mind that if the bushwhacker was ever caught and brought to justice, he, personally, would be the one to effect it.

Stuffing the sack of ammunition into his saddlebags, he wheeled, cut diagonally across the dusty street for Sudreth's, a low, square building set back somewhat from the corner. A dozen or so horses standing at the hitchrack gave a lift to his hopes. His need for hands at the Diamond G now was critical, and men hanging around a saloon at that hour of the day were generally ones without regular employment and possibly looking for work.

Pushing through the swinging doors, Tom entered. Sudreth himself was behind the bar, and as he crossed the shadowy room toward the saloon man, he took quick note of the customers. Abruptly he slowed, a sudden gust of ungovernable anger ripping through him. Bill Jacks was sitting at a nearby table indulging in a game of cards with Ed Davis, Murcer, and Pete Carver. That Ernie Tolliver, the fifth member of the gang, was not present, escaped his attention.

Face hard-set and grim, Honeymaker veered from his course and moved swiftly to the side of Diamond G's one-time foreman. He reached out, seized him by the arm. Jerking the man half around, he drove a fist into his jaw.

Jacks went over backward as a yell of surprise went up from the others. Kicking the chair aside, Tom flung a glance at Davis, let it touch also Murcer and Carver.

"Stay out of this!" he snarled, and moving in, smashed another blow to the side of Jacks's head as the man was pulling himself upright.

Tom was vaguely aware of men pushing in, shouting, forming a circle around him and Bill Jacks, of Sudreth yelling something from the end of the bar. None of it registered fully on his seething consciousness. He stood motionless, waiting now for Bill to get to his feet, watching narrowly as the husky redhead, eyes burning, wheeled to face him.

"You've done took on a man, rooster," Jacks said with a slow grin. "And you're about to get your field plowed."

He lunged, thick arms outstretched. Tom dodged to the side, landed a solid blow to Bill's chin. The redhead's charge stalled. He shook himself, pivoted, the grin no longer on his lips. Lashing out with his left, he took a long step forward. Tom again rocked away—moved straight into a hard right that set him back on his heels.

Dazed, he covered up, shielding his face with his hands as he struggled to clear his wavering senses. A knotted fist thudded into his belly, tore a gasp from his blaring mouth as he buckled forward. But the pain lifted the fog from his mind. Sucking for wind, he continued to hang there. He could hear Murcer yelling for Jacks to hurry up, finish him off. The words were like spurs raking his flanks.

Spreading his fingers, Tom peered through the open

68

spaces at Jacks. The redhead was glancing about, again grinning, savoring his moment of apparent triumph. Honeymaker came up suddenly. Backhanding the redhead across the eyes with his left, he put everything into a right that connected with Bill Jacks's jaw. The man's knees sagged, arms dropping to his sides.

Swiping at the sweat misting his vision, Tom closed in. He sent a straight left into Bill's nose, followed up with a right, again to the jaw. The redhead groaned, toppled sideways to the floor. Raging, Honeymaker bent forward, grabbed Jacks by the shirt front, and dragged him upright. Holding him at arm's length, he drew back a fist, aimed another blow at the man's chin. Bill struggled feebly.

"The hell with you," Tom said abruptly, and releasing the grip, allowed Jacks to fall back to the floor.

Breathing hard and once more brushing at the sweat clothing his face, Honeymaker turned about, moved toward the bar. His throat was dry as thistledown and he needed a drink to slake his thirst and quiet his trembling muscles.

"Look out!"

Tom threw himself to one side, instinctively dipping, pivoting, and drawing his pistol in one motion. He heard the thunder of Jacks's gun, felt a tug at his sleeve as he triggered his own weapon. Bill Jacks, on one knee, jolted as the heavy bullet slammed into him at such close range. It seemed to lift him off the floor. He twisted about in the swirling, acrid powder smoke, went down full length.

Pistol still clutched in his hand, Tom took an unsteady step toward the dead man's three friends looking on in stricken silence.

"I want you out of this town—out of this valley!" he

said in a low, croaking sort of voice. "I ever run into any of you around here again you'll answer to my gun. That clear?"

"Honeymaker!"

The harsh tension and reflex action brought Tom back around fast, weapon up and ready for use. He checked his tightening trigger finger. It was the deputy, Luke Gable. Beside him was Emory Justin. Both men stood frozen, arms raised above their heads. Hooking his thumb over the hammer of his gun, Tom released it. Lowering the weapon, he slid it into its holster. At once Gable pressed forward.

"What the hell's going on here?" he demanded.

"Been a killing, Sheriff," one of the bystanders answered, pointing at Bill Jacks.

"Figured that when I heard them gunshots," the lawman snapped, whirling to Tom. "Same as I figured you'd be mixed up in it."

"Weren't his fault," another man in the crowd said. "Leastwise the shooting part."

The deputy swore deeply, glared at Honeymaker. "Come on, I'm taking you in. Ain't standing for no killings—"

"You're not locking me up," Tom cut in coldly. "Bill drew on me."

"That's the way it was, Sheriff," the bystander who had spoken first volunteered. "They was a fighting—don't know what about. The young one there beat up the redheaded one. Then when he turned his back the redhead yanked out his gun. I hollered look out and the young one looked around just as the redhead fired. Was in too big of a hurry. He missed. The young one didn't."

Gable glanced about questioningly, settled his attention on Sudreth. "That the way it was?"

The saloon man shrugged. "Bill Jacks shot first," he admitted grudgingly.

"That satisfy you?" Tom asked harshly, moving on to the bar.

"Reckon it does," the lawman replied, and made a motion at the crowd. "Move on. This here's all over."

"Not yet, Deputy," Honeymaker called, making himself heard above the shuffling of boots. Ignoring Sudreth, he took up a bottle standing on the bar, helped himself to a drink, and then turned to the men facing him expectantly.

"I'm looking for hired hands," he said. "If you can work cows, I've got a job for you. Place is the Diamond G, northwest of here."

"What're you paying?" someone wanted to know.

"Thirty a month and found."

"Best you hear the whole thing before any of you go lining up with him," Gable warned, lifting his hand for silence. "Just be letting yourself in for a lot of trouble. He's getting all set to fight every rancher in this here valley —and what's more, that man laying dead there is his foreman."

The saloon was in complete hush for several moments and then someone said: "Is that right, mister?"

Tom took another swallow of the raw, bracing whisky, set the bottle back on the counter, and dug into his pocket for a coin.

"Close enough," he said, dropping a dollar onto the bar, and starting for the door. "If you want work, you know where to find me."

The hush resumed, followed him as he crossed the

board floor, and then just as he reached the batwings he paused, hearing Emory Justin's sighing voice.

"Ain't no doubt—we're looking at Burl Honeymaker— thirty years ago."

Tom pivoted slowly. "You're wrong," he said tightly. "You're looking at me. Understand that. I'm me, not my pa."

12

Honeymaker shouldered through the swinging doors of the saloon onto the landing. A scatter of townspeople, attracted by the sound of gunshots, were gathered in the street before the building. He met their stolid, unforgiving stares with cool indifference, and stepping down into the loose dust, strode to where the black was waiting. Without a backward look, he mounted the gelding and pulled away from the hitchrack.

Once in the saddle the high-flown tension that had gripped him from the moment he'd spotted Jacks in Sudreth's finally began to dissipate, and the full impact of what had transpired within the low-roofed structure began to hit him. He had killed a man, and the recognition of that fact was laying its restraint upon him. It was not that death was any stranger to him; in that still raw and often violent land he had seen men die—but never by his hand.

Often he had wondered what it would be like, just how it would feel to be standing over a dead man, looking down into a lifeless face while he holstered his smoking pistol. He didn't relish the thought, he found, but it hadn't sidetracked the schooling sessions with a six-gun in which Pearly Quinn had insisted he participate.

Usually his mentor had been the vaquero, Tularosa, and sometimes it was Gabe Archer or one of the more adept punchers, and on occasions he found himself under the further supervision of some still-faced, soft-spoken drifter who just happened to be a marvel when it came to the quick-draw, shoot-straight technique of handling a pistol, and who, while tarrying long enough to accumulate a stake, imparted some of his skill before riding on.

Tom reckoned he should be glad he'd spent time with each of them, that he'd learned well the lesson that a fast draw was fine but accuracy was equally important. The veracity of that axiom had been proven there in Sudreth's when Bill Jacks, who fancied himself something of a gunslinger, had relied entirely on speed and then paid the price for inaccuracy.

He sighed heavily as the black plodded slowly on in the bright sunlight. The world had changed vastly for him in slightly more than twenty-four hours. In that brief span of time his father had been cut down by a bushwhacker's bullet, had been laid in his grave, and he had become the owner of the largest and most powerful ranch in the Cibola Valley—inheriting, incidentally, the hate that went with it.

He'd already clashed bitterly with neighbors Henry Kanin, Con Mayo, and Gus McNabb after members of his crew, who subsequently walked out on him, had staged a raid on their holdings without his knowledge, further blackening the Honeymaker name and blasting his plans for ending the long-standing era of hostility that existed.

His intentions had been of the highest, but now, paradoxically, he found himself faced not with a hoped-for revival of the dormant friendship of those neighbors and townspeople, which he'd sought to inspire by offering to share his land, but with the prospect of a bloody range war and intensified hatred. And to all that he must add the fact that he had gunned down a man. . . . He guessed the solitary bright cloud in that stormy sky of trouble was the renewal of his acquaintanceship with Ellie McNabb.

It was hard to believe, harder yet to understand, but when he gave it sober thought he reckoned it was no great puzzle. They were likening him to his pa, granting him no opportunity to be himself. The words of Emory Justin, spoken as he was leaving the saloon, drove that realization home to him.

To them he was Burl Honeymaker, alive and moving among them again; making use of his gun, having his ruthless way regardless of others. No one was giving him the chance to prove that he was himself, with different ideas and beliefs, and with their combined hatred for the elder Honeymaker now boiling over, they were planning to wreak their vengeance on him.

The son was to be made to pay for the sins of the father; that was not the way it was supposed to be, Tom reflected grimly, but it appeared that such was the fact, and he could do nothing but stand firm and meet it as best he could.

He reached the end of the street, cut left onto the road that bore into the rock-studded and brush-pocked hills west of town. He'd have a long five miles of brakes before he topped out the high country and dropped into the Cibola Valley proper. It was always a hot, dusty ride and he'd be glad when it was behind him.

Roweling the black into a lope, he mopped at the sweat on his face and neck, the need to reach the ranch pushing him urgently. He knew he could not rely too heavily on the words of Kanin and the others. They had served warning they would be moving onto Diamond G range within twenty-four hours, which meant noon of the next day.

There was nothing to guarantee they would hold off that long; it would be like them to put their threat into motion that afternoon.

Just how he would go about stopping them was not clear in his mind yet. He was woefully short of help, and could probably figure on only Archer, Quinn, Tularosa, old Manuel, and perhaps one or two others still being on the job. He wondered if any of the men in the saloon had accepted his offer of work and would be showing up. It was doubtful after what Luke Gable had told them, but it didn't cost anything to hope.

The gelding began to slow on the steeper grades in the rough country. Tom endeavored to think ahead, plan the immediate future. Getting his problem with Mayo, Kanin, and McNabb settled was foremost. They would have to be stopped, made to understand that Honeymaker land could not be taken by force and that it was not for sale—and that he would fight any one of them, or all, to a standstill if they thought otherwise. Once that was established and there was no doubt in anyone's mind that he meant every bit of it, he would again make his offer simply to give them that portion of his range below Coyote Arroyo and—

The hard spanging sound of metal striking metal and a flash of pain in his left thigh brought a sudden halt to Honeymaker's contemplations. The black reared, began to pitch and wheel as the hollow, flat crack of a rifle reached Tom's ears. The bushwhacker again! His bullet had hit the saddle horn, glanced off, plowed into his leg, and passing on through, stung the gelding.

Ignoring the pain, Tom hung on, fighting to stay on the frantically bucking horse while he endeavored to locate

76

the killer in the wild tangle of brush and rock. But for what seemed an eternity the black continued to plunge and spin, making it impossible for him to do anything other than concentrate on staying in the saddle.

Finally the big horse began to tire, and hunched low, eyes searching the brush, Tom urged him toward a dense stand of scrub oak and junipers off to his left. Was it the same killer who had put a bullet into his father and later taken a shot at him? Or could it be Bill Jacks's friends, seeking to even up the score? He doubted that; there was only one man out there in the shadowy bramble, he was certain, and too, it was unlikely they thought enough of Jacks to take—

Honeymaker reeled under a powerful blow to the head. In that same fragment of time the dry crack of a rifle registered dully in his ears. He was then vaguely conscious of buckling forward, of grabbing the saddle horn with both hands—and of the black breaking into a hard run.

Ellie McNabb, much refreshed after a half hour's swim in Duck Lake, as they called the small, spring-fed pond gracing the southwest corner of the ranch, sat on a log near the edge of the water, and well hidden by tall willows, drew on her clothing.

The dip had felt good. She had spent the morning in the kitchen with her mother, baking bread and pies and cooking up a store of food for use in the coming week. When those chores and certain other household duties were done, she had felt the need to relax and cool off, and advising her mother of such, she had saddled her mare and ridden out to the pond.

It was a quiet, secluded place, one of her favorite retreats, where she could be entirely to herself and pursue her thoughts without interruption or fear of being seen. The bulk of the ranch, the range where the hired help were at work, lay to the north and east, her father having erected the house and other structures at this extreme southern end of his land so that it would be nearest and therefore convenient to the town. The fact that Duck Lake was less than a mile from the ranch house was by pure accident.

Finished with her dressing, Ellie began to plait the long, dark strands of her hair, almost dry now from the sun, and once again began to think about Tom Honeymaker and what was happening to him. She'd heard her father telling her mother of the ultimatum Henry Kanin and Con Mayo had delivered, heard him say, too, that he was having nothing to do with what they had in mind.

She was pleased that he felt that way about it. It wasn't right that Henry Kanin and Con Mayo should band together against Tom in a plan to drive him off his land simply because they hated his father. Just about everybody in the Cibola Valley hated Burl Honeymaker, she supposed, but that didn't give them the right to take it out on Tom.

She wondered what he would do. Would he give in to their demands or would he fight? She didn't know him well enough to make any kind of a prediction but she found herself hoping that somehow he would come up with enough gumption to make a stand against them.

Her father had said he'd warned them not to set foot on his range, and made it clear that he would stop them if they made any attempt; but her father had also said that he figured it was only talk, that Tom wasn't in any position to put up a fight—which was probably the truth.

How could he expect to hold off Kanin and Mayo and the two or three dozen men they could get together to do their bidding? Tom didn't even have a full crew. That Bill Jacks and those toughs that ran with him had quit, according to her father, which left him with only five or maybe six riders—all old. He'd not stand a chance.

And she believed what Tom had said about having nothing to do with the damage Bill Jacks and his bunch had done to their ranch, and to Mayo's and Kanin's. Tom wasn't that sort—she was positive of it. He was different from his father, and you'd think folks could see that. Why, he'd offered a big piece of his range to her father and the other ranchers, telling them straight out that it was land he wasn't using and didn't need. Burl Honeymaker would never have done anything like that.

But Kanin and Mayo wouldn't listen to him, had just laughed off the offer although her father said he believed it was a fine idea and that they should take Tom up on it. They turned it down cold. Truth was they didn't *want* to accept it. They figured they had a good chance to grab all of the Honeymaker land, and that's what they were going to do.

Ellie, hair now arranged to her satisfaction, stared out over the unruffled surface of the pond. A redwing black-bird, his scarlet patches brilliant in the streaming sunlight, and balanced on the head of a cattail growing along the opposite shore, was trilling cheerfully into the afternoon.

She listened to his song for a time and then sighed, wishing there was something she could do to help Tom; but she could think of no way. One thing—it might make him feel better if he knew that her father was taking no hand in what Kanin and Mayo were planning to do. Of course, he wouldn't go against them either; Angus McNabb was that way, having the old country's instincts for self-preservation, but he would keep out of it and that was something since it meant Tom would have only Mayo and Kanin to contend with.

Off to the south in the direction of a wedge of brakes country, a gunshot echoed hollowly. It was repeated shortly. Ellie considered the sound absently. Likely some drifter shooting a rattlesnake. Few persons ever rode through the area unless it was someone taking a short cut to the Honeymaker place.

She frowned at that realization, rose to her feet. A third gunshot flatted distantly, and stepping up onto the log, she tried to see above the willows to the rolling land beyond.

A horse came into view, running hard and following the trail that cut along the foot of the bluffs just west of the pond. At first she thought the horse was riderless, and then she saw that there was someone on the saddle, that whoever it was had fallen forward, was swaying from side to side while clinging desperately to the horn. The rider was badly hurt, she guessed, and then remembering the reports, probably shot.

Motionless, she watched the horse, a big black, draw near. He was coming on at top speed, evidently a runaway, frightened not only by the shooting but by the actions of the man—it looked to be a man—rocking and wobbling on and all but falling from his back. . . . And then in the distance another horse and rider raced into view.

Throat tightening, Ellie swung her attention back to the injured man. The big black he was clinging to had reached the foot of the bluffs, his sweaty coat glistening wetly as he whipped back and forth along the winding trail. He veered sharply to avoid a large rock. The man crouched on the saddle lost his grip. She saw him sail off the wildly plunging horse, go head first into the brush.

At once Ellie dropped down from the log, and pushing her way through the dense willows, hurried toward the injured man. The tightening in her throat had increased. There was something familiar about the rider.

She reached the brush, threw a glance at the black. He had not slowed but was continuing on at a mad gallop for the higher hills that lay between her father's ranch and the Honeymaker property. She could not see the second rider from where she was, but he was still approaching. The pound of his horse's hoofs was a faint tattoo in the hush.

Ellie caught sight of the fallen man in that next moment. He lay on his back, bloody face turned to the sky. The upper part of his leg, between hip and knee, also had bled profusely, soaking his cord pants and indicating a second wound. A gasp escaped Ellie's lips as she bent over the stilled figure. It was who she'd feared it would be; Tom Honeymaker.

13

She thought at first that he was dead, either from the gunshot wounds or the hard fall, and then he stirred slightly. Immediately Ellie picked up the pistol that had dropped to the ground, and sliding it back into its holster, stepped to where she could grasp him under the arms. Taking firm hold, she dragged him deeper into the brush.

Whoever it was that wanted to kill Tom Honeymaker was not satisfied he had accomplished his purpose; he was still in pursuit of the black, unaware that its rider had been thrown from the saddle.

Below a short cut-bank, and completely screened by a disorder of doveweed, ragged oak, and bush mahogany from the trail, Ellie crouched beside the wounded man, listening, nerves wire-taut, as the drumming of hoofs grew louder. She could not see the area in front of the bluffs without moving forward—and that she would not do despite a wish to know who the would-be killer was. He might notice her, and pausing to investigate or ask questions, see Tom.

The rider thundered by, loose rock on the narrow path rattling, saddle leather squeaking. Ellie kept low until the sound of the horse's passage had begun to fade and then got quickly to her feet. Tom would have to be moved to a safer place. The killer, eventually drawing near enough to the black to see that he had lost his rider, would double back, begin a search along the trail. She must have Tom well away from the area by that moment.

She gave the problem frowning consideration. It would be unwise to take him to the ranch; his presence most certainly would be noticed by one of the cowhands, even if she could keep it secret from her father, and with feeling against Tom running high in the valley, she could not afford to gamble.

But he must be where she could look after him, take care of his wounds, and where he could rest without fear of being discovered. He'd lost a lot of blood, and while it wasn't possible to tell without closer examination just how seriously he'd been hurt, he needed attention as soon as possible—attention only she could supply, since going into Rimrock for the doctor would be a mistake.

The cave . . . she'd almost forgotten about it. As a child she had gone there often to play. At the upper end of the pond, it was a well-hidden pocket gouged from the face of a high embankment that tailed off from the bluffs.

Ellie turned hurriedly, ran to where she'd left the mare, and mounting, retraced her path to Honeymaker's side. Getting him onto the horse was not going to be an easy task, she thought, but she'd manage it—somehow.

Snubbing the mare close to one of the larger brush clumps, she caught Tom under the armpits again and began to drag him toward the nervous horse. Honeymaker groaned, and when she stopped, he sat up slowly. The girl dropped to her knees before him.

"Tom! Tom! It's Ellie McNabb!"

He stared woodenly at her, eyes glazed, unseeing. Hand trembling, he reached up, touched the blood-crusted side of his head. It was a raw-looking wound just above the temple.

"Can you hear me, Tom?"

He continued to stare. Lips tight, Ellie drew herself upright. She could expect little help from him. He was only partly conscious, a man half asleep, half awake. She grasped him by an arm, tugged.

"Get up, Tom!" she shouted at him. "You have to stand up!"

A tremor of relief went through her as he half turned, struggled to his feet, left leg extended stiffly. She was reaching his consciousness.

Holding firm to his arm, she guided him, hobbling, to the mare. The horse had settled down somewhat but when Ellie, realizing he could not make use of his injured leg in mounting, brought him around to the mare's right side and attempted to get him onto the saddle, the animal began to shy.

"Tom!" Ellie shouted, putting her lips close to his ear. "You've got to help me. You've got to climb onto the saddle!"

With the horse backed against the unyielding brush, Ellie took Honeymaker's hands, placed one on the cantle, the other on the horn. Then, wrapping both her arms around his uninjured leg, she began to push upward, boosting him with all her strength.

"The saddle, Tom—get on the saddle!" she begged. "Hurry! There's no time."

Obediently, as if in a trance, he drew himself, belly flat, onto the hull. Ellie seized his right foot, squared him around until he was astride, and then pushed it into the stirrup.

Breathless, she stepped back. He was on the horse, but keeping him there while she led the mare through the tangle of brush and over the uneven ground was going to be a problem. Again she moved up close to him, pausing momentarily to listen for sounds of the killer returning. All was quiet, and taking both his hands, she placed them on the saddle horn, closed the fingers tight about the metal post.

"Tom—listen to me! I'm going to take you to my cave but you've got to hold on or you'll fall. Do you hear me?"

Slumped on the saddle, head slung forward, eyes still vacant, he made no response.

Worried, Ellie freed the mare's reins, and taking the cheekstrap of the headstall in her hand, she swung the horse slowly about, watching Tom narrowly all the while. He rocked dangerously but his hands seemed securely wrapped about the saddle horn and he was bracing himself with his good leg. He appeared to be vaguely aware of what was taking place.

Walking ahead of the mare, picking the smoothest path possible through the rank growth, Ellie moved on, glancing back every few steps to be certain he was not falling, while at the same time, listening for the beat of hoofs on the trail.

It seemed to require hours, but finally the steep, ragged face of the bluff was before her, and pulses quickening, she veered the mare toward the dark opening, barely visible now because of encroaching weeds at its base.

Leading the horse in as near as possible, she kicked aside the wind-blown accumulation of litter blocking the entrance, and pulling Tom's hands from the horn, dragged him slowly off the saddle.

She staggered under his weight, braced herself by hanging onto the mare's mane while he righted himself on his good leg, and then, placing herself under his shoulder, she assisted him, crow-hopping, into the cave. His strength was gone after that and he settled immediately onto the cool ground, still utterly quiet and with that dazed, dreamlike look on his blood-smeared, dirt-streaked face.

Straightening him out to lie full length, taking care to lift his wounded leg gently, Ellie reached under her skirt and removed her petticoat. Ripping it into two pieces, she folded one into a thin pillow, placed it beneath his head. Taking the remainder, she hurried to the pond and soaked it thoroughly in the cool water.

Back with him again, she took a portion of the wet cloth, and bathing his face and neck, removed the crust that had formed. It afforded her a close look at the wound. The bullet had grazed him, which accounted for his dazed condition. It had not cut deep, but whether it had struck him hard enough to cause permanent injury she had no way of knowing.

Placing a strip of the wet cotton cloth over the open wound, Ellie turned her attention to his leg. She was unable to get to it because of his pants, and releasing the buckles of both his belts, she pulled down one side of his trousers to where she could examine the injury. An ugly slash had been ripped across the surface of his thigh. It had bled copiously, and as she dabbed lightly at the area with a bit of the soaked cloth, it began to bleed anew.

A sigh slipped from the girl's lips. Tom was not too

badly hurt unless the bullet grazing his head had caused more damage than was apparent. But the wounds should be attended to immediately, and that meant obtaining medicine, proper bandages, along with some food and blankets. He would be weak from the loss of blood and in need of nourishment and rest.

And she must not move him. He would be safe only there in the cave beyond the reach of the man who had shot him and all of the others who would wish him dead. There was but one answer; she would make a hurried trip to the ranch, collect the necessary items, and return as quickly as possible. He could rouse, attempt to leave on his own; such could only aggravate his wounds, and there was the possibility he would fall and injure himself more severely; accordingly, she must lose no time.

Wrapping a band of the wet cloth around the gash in his leg, and securing the one she'd placed on his head wound, Ellie backtracked to where she'd left the mare. Swinging onto the saddle, she listened briefly for any indication of the killer's presence on the trail, and hearing none, set out for the ranch at a lope.

It would be necessary to take her mother into her confidence, of course. She'd never be able to gather the needed articles otherwise. Too, her absence from the house that coming night would have to be explained satisfactorily to her father. She would get her mother to say she was off visiting a girl friend—one of the families in the valley. And tomorrow night? Well, she'd think about that when it came.

14

Awareness came suddenly to Tom Honeymaker. Abruptly emerging from a depthless void, he found himself again in a state of consciousness. He was sitting on the floor of a shadowy cave. The sun was shining brightly beyond its entrance, and a girl—Ellie McNabb—was spooning thick, meaty broth into his mouth.

He stared wonderingly at her, felt a stab of pain in his left leg when he moved, glanced quickly at it. That motion brought a second spurt of pain, this time to his head. He smiled grimly at the girl.

"What the hell—"

Relief spread over her features as she set the pan of broth aside. "You're in a cave on our ranch. I brought you here."

"Brought me?"

"You got shot and fell off your horse. I had to hide you. This was the best place."

He was beginning to remember. In the brakes—on his way back to the Diamond G . . . bushwhacker. . . . He'd been hit in the leg and his horse had gone loco. . . . Before he could do much of anything another bullet had struck him. About all he could recall after that was grabbing onto the saddle horn while his horse went racing up the trail.

"How long've I been here?"

"Since yesterday afternoon."

He swore softly, glanced again to the mouth of the cave. "What time is it now?"

"Noon—a bit after, I expect. You've been unconscious until just now. I was starting to worry—afraid you weren't coming to."

Honeymaker was studying her closely. "And you've been here all that time looking after me?"

Ellie said, "Yes," and reaching into a canvas sack, produced a pint bottle of whisky. "Take a drink of this. It'll probably help."

He thanked her, pulled the cork from the container, and took a swallow. The liquor moved through him like liquid fire, and almost immediately he began to feel its lifting effect.

"Seems I owe you plenty," he said, returning the bottle to her.

"I just happened to be nearby," she replied, exchanging the whisky for the pan of broth. "You'd better eat more of this. I've been feeding it to you all night so's you could get your strength back. You lost a lot of blood."

Tension and a sense of urgency was beginning to build within him, but he took the spoon from her, began to ladle out the thick soup. There were slivers of meat floating around in it along with some kind of vegetable, and the smell was good, somewhat voiding the sharp odor of medicine that filled the cave.

"You get a look at the man who shot me?" he asked. An edge had come into his tone.

"No. Your horse kept on going and he followed it, but I was afraid to get where I could see him when he went by."

"Afraid?"

"I thought he might see me and stop—and then find you."

"Pretty sure he's the same one who killed my pa, took a crack at me right afterward. Hadn't been for that damned horse acting up, I might've seen who he was."

The pan was empty. Putting it aside, he helped himself to another drink of the whisky, glanced around at the blankets, the bottles of medicine, bandages, and items of food.

"You bring all this from home?"

Ellie nodded. He frowned doubtfully.

"Your folks will be wondering—"

"Mama knows, and we've kept it from Papa. He thinks I'm off visiting. I wasn't sure how he'd take it, so I persuaded Mama to tell a little white lie for me."

McNabb . . . McNabb, Kanin, and Con Mayo—and it was past noon. The last of the shadows in Tom Honeymaker's mind cleared in a sudden gust. At that moment they would be moving onto his range, taking it over, laying claim to his ranch. And to oppose them there would be only a handful of his men.

"I've got to get out of here," he said harshly, and started to rise.

Pain drove him back, sent a surge of nausea through him. Jaw set, he hung there, palms flat on the floor of the cave, face tipped down, sweat beading his forehead. After it had passed, he looked up at the girl, features showing the strain.

"I don't think you understand. I've got to get back to my ranch—help—"

"You're too weak," Ellie said matter-of-factly. "Maybe in a few hours—"

91

"Be too late. There's only Pearly Quinn and Archer and Tularosa, a couple others there to fight for me. Kanin and his bunch will kill them."

The girl wrung out a strip of cloth in a shallow bowl of water. Moving closer to him, she wrapped it about his head.

"They're all men who've been around for a long time and can take care of themselves. And I know they wouldn't want you doing something foolish—like trying to ride."

He stirred angrily, displacing the cloth. "They'll need me."

Ellie clamly restored the strip of wet cotton to its position. "A couple more hours won't make that much difference to them, and it will help you considerably. . . . Things may not be as bad as you think, anyway."

He looked at her sharply. "You hear something about it?"

"No, only that Kanin and Mayo were going to drive their herds onto your range."

"And your pa—"

She smiled. "He's not in on it. They're the only ones, and we can't be sure they've started. Could be they're holding off now."

The damp cloth felt good, and he fell silent thinking of what she had said. He was pleased that Gus McNabb was not a party to the move, but she was wrong where Kanin and Mayo were concerned; they would go through with it whether McNabb was with them or not. Groaning, he leaned back against the wall of the cave; there was no arguing with the girl, or with the fact that he was in no shape to do anything at the moment. He could only bide his time, rest—but only for a while.

92

"You must've had a hard time getting me here."

"You helped—some. I made you understand by yelling at you."

He looked at her curiously. "Yelling?"

"You were in a daze, not completely out of your senses, but not conscious either. That's the way you've been up until a few minutes ago."

"Lucky, I reckon, that bullet did no more than just graze me—and that you were around. Want to thank you again."

Ellie made no reply. She was staring off into the distance, eyes lost on the country beyond the pond, shimmering gently in a light breeze. Finally she stirred, turned to him.

"What are you going to do—when you leave here, I mean?"

"Get back to my place, fast," he said at once. "Told the crew to move my herd up into the Rinconada. Wanted it there where it'd be safe and out of the way and I wouldn't have to worry about it. If that's been done, then I'm going after Kanin and Mayo, drive them off my land."

"You have no help," the girl said wearily. "A half a dozen old men—stove-up has-beens, Papa called them, and nobody else will give you a hand because—"

He smiled wryly when she hesitated. "Because I'm a Honeymaker?"

Ellie nodded frankly. "You won't stand a chance against the big bunch of toughs Mayo and Henry Kanin will have backing them."

"Maybe, but it doesn't change anything. It's my ranch. I'm going to fight for it."

Her eyes met his squarely. "I want to help, Tom. I can shoot a rifle."

"Can't let you. Be too risky," he replied, his voice tighten-

93

ing a little. After a moment he added, "Seems I've just found you and I'm not about to let anything bad happen to you now."

"But alone—or almost alone, how can you—"

"I'll think of something. Got to," he said firmly, and again placing his hands on the ground, made an effort to rise.

Hope lifted within him. The pain was not so severe and there was no sickening rush of nausea. Rolling slowly onto his right leg, he doubled his knee and managed to pull himself onto it. Ellie moved quickly to his side, meaning to help. He shook her off.

"Best I do it alone—if I can," he muttered, striving to ignore the pain now shooting through his injured leg.

He paused, half kneeling, breathing hard. Then, putting his weight on his arms, extended beneath him like stiff props, he pushed himself upright. For a long moment he thought he would fall as the cave swirled around him, but that ended, and lips in a tight line, he settled himself on both feet, tested his strength.

It wasn't too bad. The wounded leg pained as he attempted to stand on it, ceased its throbbing when he shifted the load to the other. There was only a dull aching in his head. He turned his attention to Ellie.

"Think I can make it, but I'm going to need a horse."

She considered him anxiously. "Moving around like that could start the bleeding again."

"Aim to be careful. Can you get me a horse?"

The girl nodded. "At the ranch. It'll take an hour or so."

"That'll be fine. While you're gone I'll stay on my feet, get strung out. Time you're back I ought to be in shape to ride."

"I—I'm not so sure you ought to rush this—"

"No choice, unless I want to lose everything."

"Would that be so bad?"

"Maybe not far as the ranch goes, but being Tom Honeymaker, not just Burl Honeymaker's son, and needing to prove that matters plenty to me. Don't know whether that makes any sense or not."

"I guess it does," she said, and turned for the mouth of the cave. "I'll hurry."

"Ellie—"

She hesitated, and moving up to her in slow, careful steps, he took her shoulders in his hands and drew her close. Tipping his head, he kissed her on the lips.

"Not meaning that as another thank you. It's what I've wanted to do ever since you came by the house."

"And what I've been hoping you'd do," she said, eyes suddenly misty. Wheeling, she hurried out into the bright sunlight.

15

Honeymaker, left leg extended rigidly, carrying his weight on the right, glanced again at the sun. It would be around four o'clock, perhaps a bit later, he reckoned, and he was still miles from the ranch. But he could make no faster time; the horse Ellie had brought him, a husky, if elderly buckskin, was capable of more speed but Tom found it impossible to withstand the sickening increase of pain that a lope or a trot brought about.

He supposed he shouldn't complain. At least he was on the way, hours late to be sure, but he would finally get there and if luck was with him, he'd be in time.

The long, endless minutes waiting for Ellie to return with the horse had been spent well. At first he'd taken it very easy, moving about inside the cave, loosening his tight muscles and adjusting his stance to one that evoked the least discomfort.

Eventually he'd strapped on his gun and ventured outside where he hobbled back and forth across the front of the bluff, sweat pouring off him, until, when the girl returned, he was moving about with much less restriction and more confidence.

Ellie was still reluctant for him to go but she did not oppose it, and when he'd made his way to a stand upon a large rock in order to swing more easily onto the saddle, she had put her arms around him and returned his kiss.

"I'll be waiting at home for you," she said.

"Can figure on me being there no later'n tomorrow," he had promised, and settling himself on the buckskin, ridden off.

When he looked back moments later she had not yet begun to gather the blankets and other articles she'd brought to the cave but was standing on the rock following him with her eyes. He'd raised his hand and she had waved, then a bend in the trail had hidden her from view.

The knowledge that she felt toward him as he did her was filling him with a warm glow, and at the same time hardening his determination to hang on to all that was his for her sake. They could have a fine life together, and Ellie deserved the best, which, in the form of the vast, rich Diamond G, he could give her. It was just a case of driving off those who would wrest it from him. That would be accomplished somehow. Holding fast to his heritage was now more than a matter of pride, of establishing himself as a man; it meant the future for Ellie and him—and no one was going to deprive him of that.

Shifting, he eased his leg and brushed the sweat from his face. The wound in the side of his head was smarting and the dull aching had never ceased, but he scarcely noticed them. Only his leg gave him cause to worry a bit. He could not move quickly, and getting on and off a horse would be no easy task.

Too, the slightest pressure upon his thigh, from the outside as well as beneath where it rested against the saddle, caused a steady flow of pain. But he could stand it, and he would be careful, as he'd promised Ellie, not to overtax it and start the bleeding again.

Bracing himself with a hand on the cantle, Tom twisted slightly, glanced back. He was well past the bluffs now and again passing through a rough, ragged area of short, brush-filled draws, rocks, and sandy arroyos. A few squat piñon trees and thickly branched cedars were scattered about, and here and there a pine reared itself in stately splendor over the lesser growth, its parental seed having been carried down at some time in the past from higher levels by one of the wild storms that frequently lashed the mountains.

There were quite a few stray cows to be found in there, Honeymaker recalled, and a man might do well to send in a few punchers, chouse the mavericks as well as the lost branded stock into the open, and drive them back to the herd. He'd give it more thought once things settled down.

A fleeting bit of motion to his left caught at Tom's attention. Without slowing the buckskin, he fixed his eyes on the shadowy stand of brush concerned, probed it carefully. It could have been a stray, or possibly a deer, he realized; or it could have been a man on a horse.

His hand dropped to the pistol at his side. He was taking no chances this time, and while it did not seem likely it could be the bushwhacker, he would nevertheless be ready.

The buckskin plodded on, now following a well-marked game trail along the edge of a fairly wide arroyo. Being the catch basin for surrounding slopes, the area was the recipient of more than an ordinary share of water rushing down from higher levels and such bounty gave special impetus to the growth of rabbitbush, the oak brush, trees, and other shrubs usually stunted from the lack of moisture.

Thus Honeymaker's vision was restricted to only a few yards.

It would be an ideal place for an ambush, he thought, and taking his glance from the spot where he'd seen motion, he let it sweep to the sides. He saw movement again, drew up short, a coldness flooding through him. There was no mistaking what he had seen; a bay horse with one white stocking—and there was a rider.

At once Tom drew his pistol, and oblivious to the pain, jammed his spurs into the flanks of the buckskin and sent him plunging ahead. Instantly a rifle cracked, filling the canyon with rebounding echoes. Honeymaker, crouched low, threw two quick shots into the shadows where he had seen the bay disappear. Another rifle shot came in immediate response.

It was the bushwhacker—it had to be. Apparently he had doubled back the day before, and not finding the body of his intended victim, had concluded his bullets had only wounded. Then, knowing the destination Tom would take once recovered sufficiently to ride, had lain in wait.

Honeymaker swore savagely. This time he'd settle it. Cutting the buckskin about sharply, he rode down into the arroyo, and using his spurs unmercifully, drove the horse into the brush and straight toward the point where he'd last seen movement.

Branches lashed at him, slashed at his face, whipped his body. Heedless, he pressed on, pistol raised, ready to fire at the slightest excuse. The rifle barked again, now coming from hard right—and betrayed by a puff of smoke. Its bullet clipped through nearby leaves, whining slightly as it lost form on the impacts and sped on through the warm air.

Tom again fired twice at the telltale bit of gray haze, rushed on, giving the heaving buckskin no chance to slow. Once more the rifle set up its chain of echoes, this time from a maze of rocks and tall weeds farther over. It was a deadly game of hide and seek—one that he had to win, Tom thought grimly, as he again swerved the buckskin.

The brush ahead stirred. He snapped a shot, pressed the trigger for a second. The hammer clicked on an empty chamber. Cursing, he allowed the horse to veer away from the rocks, and flipping open the loading gate of the pistol, began to rod out the spent cartridges and reload, filling all six chambers in the cylinder.

Jerking hard on the leathers, he cut the horse back toward the rocks, eyes straining for a sign of the rifleman. He reached the mound, roweled the buckskin into its center. A rabbit seeking cover from the confusion, darted into the open space between two large boulders. Reacting instantly, Tom snapped a bullet at the bit of gray and white fur, showering dirt upon it as it scampered away. He swore tautly, rode on.

The jumble of rocks sloped off, merged into a deep hollow gray-green with buffalo grass. At once Honeymaker drew in the buckskin. To continue would be foolhardy. Beyond the shelter of the brush and rocks he would become an easy target from all sides.

Glancing around, he wheeled, faded back into the maze. The rifle cracked the late afternoon hush instantly. He'd been right once more; the bushwhacker was waiting, expecting him to step into his trap.

Again the rifle fired. The buckskin shied violently as the bullet shrilled off a rock near his head, reared. Tom, taken unawares, slid back over the saddle's low cantle. He grabbed frantically for the horn, saving himself from a bad fall but dropping his pistol in the process.

The buckskin steadied, and leg screaming with pain, Honeymaker bent low, scooped up the fallen weapon, and settled himself. As he brought his mount back around, the steady beat of a horse coming up fast on the trail from the bluffs reached him. Frowning, he threw a glance toward the sound. Moments later a quick hammer of hoofs racing off into the opposite direction announced the departure of the bushwhacker. He, also, had heard the approaching rider.

Honeymaker shrugged wearily. Sleeving the sweat from his eyes, he pointed the buckskin toward the arroyo. Whoever it was had frightened off the killer, Tom had lost his third chance to have it out with the man who had slain his father and was seeking to take his life, too.

Glum, dissatisfied, body ravaged with pain, he rode into the wash and swung up onto the trail, attention fixed on the narrow path. The horse and rider raced into view. Tom swore feelingly. It was Ellie.

16

Sharp words formed on Tom Honeymaker's lips, dying when he saw the worry in the girl's eyes. She pulled to a halt beside him, searched his face anxiously.

"Are you all right?"

He nodded. "Was that bushwhacker again. Waited for me to come along."

Ellie was off the mare and hurrying to him, glance on his wounded leg. "You're bleeding. I'll try to stop it."

Tom dismounted stiffly and she at once began to fuss with the leg of his trousers. Impatient, he reached for his belt knife, and in a quick motion, slashed the fabric in order that she might more quickly get to the injury.

"I heard the gunshots and was afraid you'd run into trouble," she said, adjusting the compress that had worked out from under the bandage encircling his thigh. "This ought to be changed—a clean pad—"

"Can't spare the time," he cut in, gruffly.

Ellie stepped back. "It will probably do for a while, if you're careful. . . . Did you see who it was?"

"Jasper on a bay. Horse had one white stocking—left hind leg. Pretty sure it was the same man that took a shot at me the day Pa was killed."

"Does that help any?" she asked. "I mean—a bay horse

with one white stocking, does it belong to somebody you know?"

Honeymaker shook his head. "No, but I've got a pretty good idea who it is. Mentioned that when I was talking to Kanin and Con Mayo, and your pa, yesterday. Said I'd be looking him up. Looks like he's out to get me before I can get him."

"Who do you think it is?"

Tom gave that thought for a long minute while he leaned against the buckskin, favoring his leg. He wasn't certain, of course, and he didn't like expressing his belief until he had proof. But if anything went wrong Ellie had the right to know.

"Joe Kanin."

The girl stared at him. "Are you sure?"

"No," he said flatly. "Only saying that I think he's the one. Henry Kanin dropped by to talk right after Pa was murdered. Joe wasn't with him. Always before you'd see them together out on the range. He showed up the next day when we had that meeting."

"Hard to understand why he—"

"Probably figured he was helping out his pa, doing him a good turn getting rid of the man who stood in his way. Best we mount up. Losing daylight."

Ellie reached for the buckskin's bridle, held the horse still while Tom swung awkwardly onto the saddle from the right-hand side, and then, hurrying to the mare, climbed aboard.

"I guess it could be," she said in an uncertain voice, "but Joe never struck me as having that much spunk."

"Don't take much getup to shoot a man in the back,"

HONEYMAKER'S SON

Tom said dryly. "See you tomorrow," he added, and put the buckskin into motion.

"I'm coming with you."

Tom halted abruptly as the girl rode in behind him. Face stern, he said: "My ranch'll be no place for you when the trouble starts."

"It's where I should be when it does," she replied quietly, and nodded at the lowering sun. "Be dark soon. We'd better hurry."

Honeymaker did not move but the set of Ellie's mouth was firm, stubborn. "I don't like it," he said finally. "If you come you're promising right now to do exactly what I tell you."

She nodded. "I just want to be with you."

He turned back at that and together they rode off along the trail, silence hanging between them. A time later she spoke, evidently noticing they were bearing steadily into the southwest and not toward the north for the Rinconada.

"Headed for the ranch," he said to her question. "Got to see if they've moved in on me yet."

It was full dark when they reached the cluster of buildings and drew up behind the windbreak at the end of the ranch house. Light shown only in its west windows, the bunkhouse and all else being dark and apparently deserted.

Easing off the buckskin, Tom handed the reins to the girl. "Won't be more'n fifteen minutes. If something happens and I don't show up, ride to the Rinconada. Pearly and the others'll look after you."

"I'll just wait," Ellie murmured in that quiet, unyielding way he was learning to associate with her.

"Twenty minutes—then, by God, move out," he snapped,

equally obstinate, and keeping close to the side of the house, began to work his way to the rear.

He saw three horses standing at the hitchrack, heard voices when he came to the corner. Drawing up close to the wall, he studied the figures visible in the fan of light a lamp was spreading on the porch and into the yard. Two men were slouched in chairs; a third, tip of his cigarette glowing, hunkered on his heels, back against one of the roof supports.

Careful to make no sound, Tom slipped in closer. He could not distinguish any of them in the weak light and their voices were too low to be recognizable. Reaching a clump of bush briar, he again paused. It would be too risky to get any nearer.

"This here'll make a mighty good place to headquarter out of—"

It was Henry Kanin. Bristles lifted on Honeymaker's neck. His hand dropped to the pistol at his hip, fell away. Making any sort of play now would be foolish, and with the odds three to one, maybe fatal.

"For a fact . . . what about Mayo? You figure he'll stand still for us taking it over?"

The voice was that of Lou Cobb, the Box K's foreman.

"Hell with Mayo. You seen him today?"

"Nope. Expect he's with his herd, howsomever. Man don't believe in hiring a foreman, does the work hisself."

"Was a lot of stock coming up from the east. Guess that's his."

"What it is. Must be close to a thousand head in the bunch. Be driving in the rest tomorrow, I reckon."

Kanin yawned. "Joe doing all right?"

"He is, far as I know. Put him in charge of the bunch of

cows we had grazing below the hogback. Told him to start drifting them north."

"The boy'll do fine," Kanin said, and yawned again. "I want all my stock on Honeymaker range by noon tomorrow, Lou."

"Most of it's already there—leastwise over the line—"

"But you ain't got none of it past Coyote Arroyo yet."

"Nope. Expect to be crossing it sometime in the morning."

"Well, head them up early. Sooner we get the whole herd—and Mayo's—up to the Rinconada, better I'll like it."

"Sure, Mr. Kanin," Cobb said, pulling himself upright. The puncher hunched against the post, flipped his dead cigarette into the dark, also came to his feet. "You staying the night here?"

Kanin rose. "No, I'm going home. Tomorrow you send a couple of the boys over here. Have them drag out all the stuff inside the house, excepting the furniture, pile it in the yard and burn it. . . . Don't go forgetting it, now."

"Won't," Cobb said, and with the puncher beside him, stepped down from the porch and crossed to his horse. "Night," he called back.

"Night," Kanin answered, and started toward his own horse.

Anger pushing at him, Tom watched the three men get onto their mounts, ride silently side by side for the width of the yard, and then disappear into the night.

Kanin had taken over, had moved in and was laying claim to the house. Tomorrow he planned to have its

contents carried into the yard and a torch applied. . . .
The hell he would! He'd not touch a finger on one—

Honeymaker caught at his soaring anger, brushed at
his face. It was no time to lose his head; it was the time
to do some hard thinking. He'd learned several things, the
most important of which was that Kanin and Mayo
cattle, while on Diamond G range, were still below
Coyote Arroyo. They'd not made much progress toward
occupying his land as yet. Evidently moving the herds
had not gotten underway until around noon, perhaps after.

That was good. It fit well into a scheme that was now
beginning to take shape in his mind—a plan that called for
a show of raw, ruthless power and wholesale destruction,
the only things that Henry Kanin and Con Mayo under-
stood. They might have the men, the willing gunfighters,
but he had the equalizer.

Wheeling, limping badly, Tom turned to rejoin Ellie.
A deep satisfaction was filling him. Mayo and Kanin
thought that by overrunning him they could drive him
out. That was a mistake. They were going to learn that
a Honeymaker was always a Honeymaker.

17

He was quiet as they rode steadily northward through a narrow valley that broke the otherwise flat grassland. The stars were out and a three-quarter moon lit up the sky and spread a pale glow over the countryside, giving all things a soft-edged, gentle look. Coyotes barked in the short hills and somewhere far to the west a gunshot flatted through the warm hush.

There was a difference in him, Ellie realized. In only those few minutes that he had been away from her a change had taken place. He seemed to have hardened, stiffened and there was now a resoluteness to him that was almost sullen. It was as if he had reached some crossroad in his life while standing there in the darkness beside the house that had always been his home, and chosen a course, one not to his liking but that was necessary.

"Back—at your ranch," Ellie said, breaking the silence hesitantly, "was it so bad?"

He stirred on his saddle. "No, not yet."

"Who was there?"

"Kanin and Lou Cobb. One of their hired hands."

His replies were clipped, to the point. But he needed to talk, relieve the anger that was trapped within him, and being a woman with the understanding of her kind, Ellie recognized the fact.

"Joe wasn't with them?" she probed, gently.

That seemed to break down the barrier. His shook his head. "Cobb told Kanin he'd put him to working cattle early this morning on their lower range."

"Then—if he was there maybe he wasn't the one who—"

"Thought of that. Cobb didn't see him doing it, just told him to. It would've been easy for Joe to show up for the rest of the help to see, then ride back to the bluffs, hang around waiting for me so's he could finish the job he'd started—and get back before he was missed."

"I've never been down there. I don't know how much of a ride it would be."

"He could do it easy enough," Honeymaker said, and then in a tight voice added: "They've moved their herds onto my range. Tomorrow they're aiming to cross Coyote Arroyo and start a drive to the Rinconada. They'll never get there—never."

Ellie considered his set features in the half dark. "How can you stop them?"

"There's a way," he replied and let it drop.

They pressed on through the calm, pleasant night, the horses traveling at a leisurely gait. The irregular outline of the higher hills silhouetted against the sky was becoming more distinct now and Ellie guessed they were drawing near the Rinconada where his crew would be camped. She hoped it would not be much farther; she could see that the wound in his leg was paining him, was certain it needed attention.

"Kanin was sitting in Pa's chair on the porch," he said

abruptly in a bitter tone. "Big as you please—like he owned the place. Says he's going to make it his headquarters."

She searched for the right words to temper the fury lying beneath his statement. "It was only talk—"

"He figures to do it in the next couple of days. He told Cobb to send over some of the hired hands, take everything out of the house but the furniture, pile it in the yard, and burn it. Means all my pa's things—and Ma's. Mine too." He paused, his torso a stiff, outraged shape in the night. "I'll see him in hell first!"

"He's only hoping to do that," Ellie said quickly, but her own indignation had risen swiftly. "A lot can happen to make him change his mind."

"Can bet on that. I'll see to it, myself . . . was all I could do back there to keep from pulling my gun and killing him on the spot. Pa and me weren't very close. I've got to admit that, but seeing Henry Kanin in his chair and hearing him brag about what he was going to do was damn near more'n I could swallow."

The fact that he had maintained control of himself when it would have been easy to obey his impulses was a tribute to him, Ellie thought. Like his father, Tom feared nothing, but unlike him he lacked the ruthlessness that characterized the older man. Or did he? She gave that deep consideration. Was it still true—or was that the change she sensed in him?

Ellie tried to analyze her feelings toward him if such was the case. Could she continue to love him if he was becoming another Burl Honeymaker—a man who would either be feared or hated by everyone? Was happiness possible under such circumstances?

She supposed she could not blame him for changing; to see another man take over his home, to hear the interloper speak of destroying the accumulation of remembrances, of family valuables, of mementos that linked preceding generations; to know that his land was being trespassed upon and would be wrested from him was more than sufficient cause.

But she did not like to think of him as being another Burl Honeymaker. It meant for him a life of constant watchfulness, of forever being alone, of trusting nobody and having no one to turn to except her once they were husband and wife—and that, too, could now change. It would be like him to avoid any such union, not wanting to bring worry and grief to her.

She, of course, had not known Tom's mother. Her own mother had said Glory Honeymaker was a beautiful and gentle woman, all but worshiped by her husband, and who had considerable influence over him. Burl was always a hard, driving sort of man, she'd said, but after Glory died giving birth to Tom, he'd become the iron-fisted, despotic tyrant Ellie'd grown up hearing about.

Had Glory lived things might have been different, her mother believed, but she wasn't sure of it. No man in the Cibola country had ever burned with the soaring ambition, the sheer need for land and cattle, and the desire for raw power that filled Burl Honeymaker. He was of a different breed, one whose hunger to own, to control, was insatiable.

It was difficult to think of Tom being that way. True, they were barely acquainted; except for the years when they were children attending grade school, and after that his infrequent appearances at church on Sunday or the Tuesday Evening Sociables, she'd seen very little of him.

The visit made to the Honeymaker ranch by her mother and herself when they heard of Burl's death was the first time she'd spoken to him in years. She had noticed him in town on a few occasions but it had just been in passing and there had been no conversation.

Ellie guessed that really didn't matter. No long period of time was required for two persons to discover they were in love if, in the beginning, they were meant for each other. Such could happen in only hours—even minutes. That's how it was with Tom and her—at least it would seem so, or had earlier, anyway. Now she wasn't so—

"Rinconada's just ahead," she heard him murmur.

18

"You will go no farther, *señor*."

The voice reaching out to them from a cluster of cedars was mild, easygoing, yet carried an unmistakable warning. And it was a familiar one.

"It's all right, *compañero*," Tom said. "It's me—and Ellie McNabb."

"Ah-h-h." The vaquero's response was a long sigh as he rode up to them. "We have worried for you, *patrón*."

Patrón. It was no longer *muchacho*, Tom realized with a hard smile. In the eyes of the Mexican he'd graduated from being a boy on the Diamond G to its boss.

"The wound—it is bad?" the vaquero asked, pointing at Tom's bandaged leg as they slanted toward a glow of firelight beyond a shoulder of rock pushing out from the low hills.

"A mite sore. It was that bushwhacker again—he almost got me. Hadn't been for Ellie he probably would've. . . . Everything all right here?"

"*Sí, patrón*. We have moved in all of the cattle and horses. A camp has been made by the rocks."

"Good. How many men have we got?"

"Only a very few, I fear," Tularosa murmured as they continued toward the ragged formation.

Several figures were grouped before the low fire, and

farther over the outline of a canvas-topped chuck wagon showed whitely in the flickering glare.

"It is the *patrón* and a lady," the vaquero called softly as they approached the camp.

The men who had wheeled quickly at the sound of the horses approaching, relaxed. Pearly Quinn and Archer came forward, both grinning broadly.

"Plenty glad to see you, son," the old cook said, reaching out a hand. "When that horse of your'n come in, blood all over the saddle, we got to thinking that bunch of Bill Jacks's must've caught up with you."

"Come morning we figured to start looking for you," Archer added, also extending his hand.

Tom accepted their welcomes gravely, swung carefully off the buckskin. He turned to the girl, already dismounting, aware of the coolness she was being accorded by the crew.

"Reckon you all know Ellie," he said, ignoring their attitude. "Her pa's Gus McNabb."

A few moments of silence followed and then Gabe Archer said, "Ain't he siding Mayo and Kanin in this here—"

"No, pulled out of it and has nothing to do with it. And it wasn't Bill's outfit that jumped me, it was that bushwhacker, taking a turn at me again. . . . How'd you know about Bill Jacks?"

"Tolliver. He's here. Quit Bill and them others after the stunt they pulled. He's wanting his old job back."

Tom and Ellie halted before the fire. Coffee was warming in the big branding-camp pot at its edge, and the smell of stew in the Dutch oven setting nearby filled the night.

He nodded, remembering. Tolliver hadn't been in the saloon at the time of his fight with Jacks. Such had passed fleetingly through his mind and he guessed he'd just assumed the man was elsewhere in the building.

"Sure glad to see you—and you, ma'am."

It was Jim Heston. Tom bucked his head at the rider, heard Ellie make her response as he let his glance run over all of the men now lined up and facing him. Old Manuel, grinning toothily, Archer, Heston, Pearly Quinn, Tularosa, and Tolliver. Six men, plus himself; six guns, since Manuel could be relied upon to do no more than stay with the cattle. . . . It wasn't much of a force with which to go against Kanin and Mayo and the small army they'd have with them, he thought heavily.

"We're plumb forgetful of our manners, I reckon," Quinn said, stepping by him. Kneeling beside the fire, he looked up at Ellie. "Ma'am, can I get you some of this here son-of-a-gun and a little coffee?"

Ellie smiled. "Your stew smells good, Pearly. I'd like to have some. Coffee, too. It's turning cold."

At once the cook took up a tin plate, cup-dipped out a generous portion of the thick mixture from its blackened iron container. Tularosa stepped up, hung a wool blanket around the girl's shoulders. She smiled at him, accepted the plate from Quinn, and thanked both.

"Will you heat some water for me?" she said then.

"Sure enough . . . you wanting to wash or something?"

"It's Tom's leg. It's been bleeding and needs dressing again."

Quinn turned away, filled a small kettle from a canteen, and set it over the flames. "Won't take more'n a couple, three minutes."

"There something else happen after that bushwhacker shot you?" Archer asked, frowning.

"He tried again when I was crossing that big wash at the foot of Skull Peak," Honeymaker said. "Was ready for him that time."

"You get him?"

"No, but I got to take a few shots at him. First time I never even had a chance to draw my gun. Don't think I hit him, but I got a good look at his horse. Was a bay."

"Bay?" Archer repeated. "That's what that jasper was riding that fired a shot at you the day your pa was killed."

"That's what I'm getting at. Pretty sure it's the same man. Pearly, give me a cup of that java. I'll pass up the son-of-a-gun—not hungry. You find the shells I had on the black?"

"Yep. They're there in the wagon," Archer said. "Had the boys take what they was needing. You looking for trouble right away?"

"Not looking for it—going to make it," Tom said, taking a swallow of the coffee. He glanced at Ellie. She had stepped back slightly, the stew on her plate only partly eaten, and was staring into the fire. "I rode by the ranch on the way here. Kanin was there."

"You meaning he's already moved in? We figured he'd take a—"

"Not exactly. Lou Cobb and some puncher was with him. Found them on the porch."

"They spot you?"

"No, kept in the dark and listened. Kanin aims to take over the place, use it for his headquarters. They've already moved cattle onto my range."

118

Quinn swore softly. Tularosa wagged his head. "That is very bad."

"What're you figuring to do about it?" Tolliver asked.

"Stop them," Honeymaker said promptly, studying the puncher carefully. "Nobody's taking my ranch away from me."

"Ain't many of us," Tolliver said, "and what I seen of Kanin and Mayo's outfits, there'll be a plenty of them."

"You're not telling me something I don't already know. But there's a way we can turn them back."

A long silence followed. Finally Jim Heston said, "Whatever it is, I reckon you'd best let us in on it."

"Just this. They'll be bringing the herd up from the south, past that wooded section where we put out the salt licks last fall. Lots of big cottonwood trees there, along with thick brush. We'll fight Indian style—hide out and pick off Kanin and Mayo's hired hands when they come by."

Again there was a hush. Tom considered the stolid faces of his crew. They were not looking at him but had their eyes on the fire, doubt and uncertainty definite in their bearing. He did not turn to Ellie, unwilling to see her reaction.

"I figure once we've blasted a half a dozen or so of them off their saddles, the others'll start pulling back. Be our chance then to get the cattle to milling so's we can turn them. We use our guns, it ought to be easy to break them into a stampede."

"Kanin and Con Mayo ain't going to be sleeping all that time," Pearly Quinn said slowly. "What's to keep them from taking a half a dozen or so of them gunnies they've got working for them, circle the woods, and come in on us from behind?"

"Nothing, except us keeping a sharp eye out for them doing it. We're going to have to keep moving all the time, staying out of sight in the bushes and among the trees. Once we've got the cattle headed the other way, we've got them licked."

Honeymaker let his words hang, have their effect. Then, "Big thing now is I've got to know again where you all stand. Each one of you'll have your part to do—there being only six of us and maybe thirty or so of them. . . . Now, I won't hold it against any man that decides to pull out. Just want to know who'll be siding me."

Quinn shrugged his slight shoulders. "Ain't so sure it'll work, but I expect you've thought it through and know what you're talking about . . . count me in."

"No sense asking me," Archer said. "Reckon you knew already how I'd feel."

"Same here," Heston murmured.

Tom shifted his attention to Tularosa. The vaquero smiled. "No man lives forever, *patrón*."

Manuel, still grinning, nodded vigorously. "You'll have to stay with the herd, *amigo*—you and the lady," Tom said, and settled his attention on Tolliver. "Haven't heard you speak up yet."

The rider pulled off his hat, scratched at his head. "Well, I reckon I ain't as brave as them other boys. I'm going to pass. Could be what you're planning—laying a ambush there in the woods—'ll work out all right, but it looks to me like you're going to be bucking for the graveyard. Now, meaning no offense, Tom, but was it your pa calling

the shots I'd not back off. I'd know for danged sure it'd
work, else he'd not be aiming to do it, but you—"

"You figure I can't pull it off, that it?"

Tolliver drew on his hat, brushed at the brim to straighten
it out. "Yep, about what it comes down to."

"And you're quitting?" Archer asked.

The puncher nodded. "Real sorry I'm feeling the way
I am, but that's how I'm looking at it, and a man's got to
be honest with hisself."

"For sure," Honeymaker said. "Expect you'll want to
ride out now. Be no sense in you hanging around here,
losing your sleep."

"Ain't it the truth," Quinn murmured. "And who
knows? Old Henry Kanin and his boogeymen just might
take a notion to start shooting at us right this minute!"

The scorn was not lost on Tolliver. He shrugged,
turned toward the horses, tied to a rope stretched between
a wheel of the wagon and a nearby cedar tree.

"So long," he said, moving off into the half dark.

No one replied to his farewell. They simply stood in
silence as he freed the reins of his mount, swung onto the
saddle, and loped away into the night.

"Sort of makes a fellow breathe easier with him gone,"
Archer said quietly, squatting by the fire and reaching for
the coffee. "Ain't never liked him none."

Tom turned to Ellie. She was staring at him, a frown
on her face. She was still thinking of the plan he'd out-
lined, considering what it meant—the cold-blooded killing
of many men whose only crime was that they worked
for Henry Kanin or Con Mayo.

He'd hoped she would think more highly of him, but

it was Pearly Quinn who saw through it all. The old cook rose suddenly, walked to the edge of the fire's glow to look off across the land in the direction Tolliver had ridden. The beat of the rider's horse was fading gradually.

"Reckon we're shed of him," Quinn said, coming back. "Safe now to tell us what you've really got on your mind."

Heston's head came up. "You mean you figured you couldn't trust that Tolliver and was just stringing him along?"

Tom nodded. "Maybe I'm wrong, and we sure could use an extra man, but my guess is he's working for Mayo or Kanin—or will be before morning."

"And that hiding out in the woods ain't what you're planning to do?"

"Got a different idea. Tell you about it while the lady patches up my leg again," Honeymaker said, coming about to face Ellie. "That is—if she won't mind."

The girl, relief showing on her features, moved toward him. "Whenever you're ready," she said, handing the plate and cup to Quinn.

19

Heavily armed, they rode out several hours before first light, Honeymaker, Gabe Archer, Quinn, Tularosa, the vaquero, and Jim Heston. Manuel and Ellie McNabb stayed behind, their job being to look after the herd. There should be no need for them to do anything, but it served as a means for keeping the girl out of harm's way and satisfied the aged yard hand's wish to be of help.

"Best we come into the ranch from the corrals," Tom said, as they hurried on through the cool, early hours. "Don't think Kanin or Mayo have moved in any of their crew but we won't take any chances."

"Your leg—how's it doing?" Quinn asked, noting the stiffness with which Honeymaker was sitting his saddle.

"No trouble," Tom answered.

Ellie had cleaned the wound, applied more of the searing ointment she had brought from home, and wrapped clean bandages about it. That she had the jar of medicine now was a matter of accident; when she heard the gunshots that day before, soon after he'd left the cave, Ellie was in the act of loading the supplies into her saddlebags preparatory to returning to the ranch. At the sound of the shooting she had quickly mounted and followed.

"That there bushwhacker," Archer said, "was on a bay horse, you was telling. It look like somebody's we know?"

Tom cocked his hat more to one side. The wound in his head, also freshly bandaged, did not pain him except when the weight of his headgear pressed against it.

"Could be, but I couldn't say. Had a white stocking, left hind leg. I never got close enough to see the brand."

"Plenty of bays around," Quinn said. "Sure too bad you couldn't see who was riding him."

"He was mighty careful to keep me from it. Ellie didn't get a look at him either."

"You thinking what I am—that he's the same jasper that shot your pa?"

"Never figured anything else. Soon as we get that herd turned back, I'm going after him."

Tom felt the eyes of the men swing to him in surprise. Jim Heston leaned forward, face intent.

"That mean you know who it is?"

"I have a strong hunch it's Joe Kanin."

"That young whelp!" Quinn exclaimed, amazed. "Didn't figure he had enough guts to ride in the dark!"

"Still how it looks to me. I'm not sure yet, though, but I'll find out before this is over with. Right now our problem's to take care of his pa and Con Mayo, and drive them off my land. Then I'll see to him. . . . Gabe, you remember how much of that blasting powder's left in the tool shed?"

"About a dozen cans, near as I recollect. Ain't used none since we cleaned out that water hole over on the west side."

"We'll pick up two cans apiece. That'll give us enough to plant clear across the break in Coyote Arroyo where the cattle will be going to cross."

"Sort of narrow in there, won't take much—"

"Know that, but we want a lot of noise and flash. Besides, we'll have to use some for fuse strings."

"From what you heard Kanin telling Cobb, all their stock ain't been brought up yet. When we set off the charges we'll only be scaring back part of the cattle, and there won't be no chance to plant more powder, even if we had it."

"Won't be necessary. All we've got to do is turn that herd," Tom said, his voice low and hard. "Once that's done, cattle coming up behind them will get caught in the rush and run with them."

"Then what?"

Honeymaker gave that several moments' thought. "It depends on what Kanin and Mayo do. If they put everybody to trying to stop the stampede, we won't have anything to do but get to the ranch. Could pan out, however, that they'll send some of their hands after us."

"If they've got any that's able," Heston said. "Best you remember that most of them'll be trailing along behind the herd, and once them cows get headed back the other way they're going to be mighty busy keeping from getting run over."

"I'm planning on that, but Kanin's going to be riled plenty. Same goes for Con Mayo—and I think we'd better play it safe and look for them to come after us."

"That is wise," Tularosa said, breaking his usual silence.

"We line out for the Rinconada?" Heston asked.

"No, head for the ranch soon as the stampede starts. It's our best bet if they follow us."

"Place for us to be, sure enough," Quinn said. "Can't think of no better place to make a stand. Some of us can get inside the house, rest of us in the barn or maybe the bunkhouse. We can pretty well cover the whole works that way."

"Going to have to watch out for them starting fires, too. Be like them to try and burn down everything."

Honeymaker nodded. He was pleased they were taking over, making suggestions as to what must be done. He felt he could not ask them to lay their lives on the line for him, that it was a decision they should make themselves, for the chances they would all survive the coming hours were somewhat less than even, all depending more or less on how the two ranchers reacted when their herds were stampeded.

If they put their efforts to halting the panicked cattle and ignored all else, matters would probably work out to where no one from the Diamond G got hurt, unless by accident. But if they decided instead to turn the situation into an all-out showdown fight designed to once and for all erase the Honeymaker name and all those who stood by it from the Cibola country, it would be war to a finish.

He would have to take it as it came. He'd worked out his strategy as thoroughly as he could, doing all possible with only four men to rely upon—even allowing for mistakes and taking steps to prevent them. But there was no way of anticipating exactly what Henry Kanin and his partner in their scheme to take over the Diamond G, Con Mayo, would do in those first minutes. If they bent their efforts to saving their cattle, the prospect was good.

If, however, thrown into a rage, they ignored the stampede, called together a number of riders and set out immediately to take vengeance on him and his crew, it would be a different matter. A running gun battle would be the result and the only hope for him and his men would be to reach the ranch house where they could fort up inside its thick walls.

Tom slowed, coming to a halt at the first of the corrals laying west of the yard and its scatter of buildings, now looming up in the dark.

"I will look," Tularosa murmured, and moved off into the shadows.

In only moments the vaquero returned. "There are horses, *patrón*. Six in number. They stand at the bunk-house."

Kanin or Mayo. One of them had apparently decided to make use of Diamond G facilities that very night, quartering men on the place where they would be available that next morning. It was a break Honeymaker had not planned on.

"We're getting lucky," he said quietly. "Ride in close but don't get so near that the horses will give us away. Then we go inside, make them a little less comfortable."

"Fix them so's tomorrow they won't be working, that it?" Quinn asked, grinning.

"Just what I mean. Take along some rope so's we can tie them up. Whoever they're hired out to will be a half a dozen men short on the drive."

It was easy. The punchers were sleeping soundly, their snores filling the bunkhouse. Leaving it to the crew, Tom stood back, watched while they closed in, bound and gagged the surprised riders—all Kanin Box K hands it developed, sent there to be ready to help with the herd when it reached that point—and sat them against the back wall of the structure.

Taking their weapons to the main house where they

could be of use later, Tom and the vaquero doubled back to the tool shed where Archer and the others were loading up with cans of blasting powder.

"There's a few cans left—maybe a half a dozen," the older man said. "I ain't real anxious to strike a match in there to find out just how many, but—"

"Two apiece will be enough," Tom said, holding open his saddlebags while Heston jammed the containers into the pockets. "How about matches—we all got plenty?"

There was a few moments of searching about while a check was made. All reported an ample supply.

"Time we moved on then," Honeymaker said, glancing toward the east. "I want these cans planted and powder strings laid and ready ahead of daylight."

An hour or so later the job was completed. All ten of the corrugated containers had been placed along the arroyo's opposite side in that section where the bank sloped down to afford an entrance, and strings of powder trailed across to nearby clumps of brush where each man would hide while awaiting the arrival of the cattle.

When the lead steers came to the edge of the broad wash, halted and prepared to drop off the shallow bank onto the arroyo's sandy floor, then and only then would the fuse strings be lit.

"It's going to blow right up in their faces," Pearly said as they moved back. "Sure'll be one hell of a fracas, all them cows trying to turn around and start running at the same time."

"Ain't nobody going to be looking for something to happen down here, neither," Heston said, "not if Tolliver went trotting back to Kanin with what you told him."

"Expect he did, all right," Gabe Archer added, his

voice filled with satisfaction. "Sure would like to be stand-ing around where I could see old Henry's face when all that powder goes off."

Tom shrugged. "Let's just hope it'll keep him busy long enough to let us get away from here," he said soberly.

20

The pearl glare in the east was changing slowly to coral. Tom, hunched behind a clump of rabbitbush, drew his brush jacket closer as he endeavored to ward off the pre-dawn chill. His leg was bothering him, and several times he'd been forced to rise and stretch in order to relieve the pain.

A dozen strides to his right, in the next bit of cover, he could see Tularosa shifting about also, easing his cramped muscles and endlessly smoking brown-paper cigarettes. He kept the slim cylinders carefully cupped inside a hand to prevent the red glow of their tips from being noticed should a Kanin rider or one of Mayo's Walking M punch-ers happen to be in the area and glance in his direction.

Elsewhere, at intervals along the arroyo, Quinn, Heston, and Gabe Archer were also waiting, hidden by brush, a large rock, or a thick clump of cedar, whichever could provide the necessary protection. They had covered the fairly wide break in the embankment of the wash down which the cattle would come very well, he saw, as the light gradually strengthened.

There would be a short distance at its upper end where no explosion of sand, leaves, dead branches, and all other litter they'd been able to collect and pile upon the cans of blasting powder, would not occur. But he was unconcerned; the cattle would not be permitted to enter the broad arroyo, and an eruption along most of the egress would turn back all of the steers in the herd's front rank.

A jack rabbit, tall, black-tipped ears erect, hopped leisurely into view, coming from somewhere below Pearly Quinn, the last in line. Heston picked up a pebble, tossed it at the animal. Startled, it bounded away on its powerful legs, leaped the wall of the wash, and disappeared into the brush.

At once Heston rose, made a quick examination of the fuse string of black powder leading to the container of explosive under his care to make certain the jack, in passing, had not disrupted it with his elongated feet. The line was apparently undisturbed and the slow-talking, leathery cowhand returned to his position.

The minutes dragged by with the air increasingly sharp while the sun continued to linger below the eastern horizon. A coyote crossed the wash, nose to the ground, short brushlike tail extended stiffly. Crows set up a raucous calling in the trees back in the direction of the ranch, and off to the west, high overhead, buzzards were circling lazily. The cattle should be moving up, Tom thought, in the relentlessly increasing tension. They should be hearing sounds of the herd's approach.

"You reckon Kanin and them've gone and changed their minds?" Gabe Archer asked in a hoarse whisper. "Figured they'd be here long before now . . . sun's up."

"They'll come," Honeymaker replied.

Abruptly a rider became silhouetted on the flat above the arroyo. Reins hooked over the horn of his saddle, he sat broadside to them, chafing and blowing into his hands in an effort to promote warmth.

"Have a care—" Tularosa warned softly, taking no chance on the others not seeing the man.

The puncher, broad-brimmed hat pulled down over his eyes to shield them from the increasing glare, remained for several minutes. Finally, taking up the leathers, he wheeled the gray he was riding sharply about and spurred off toward the south.

A faint sound began to carry through the stillness. At first it was no more than a low rumbling, and then as it grew louder, became a solid pounding, the bawling of cattle carried to Honeymaker. He smiled tightly. The herd was coming at last, and Lou Cobb, complying with Kanin's order to get his stock across Coyote Arroyo and well on their way to the Rinconada as early as possible, was keeping them on the run.

Tense, he crouched in the brush, a half a dozen matches in his hand, a small stone nearby upon which he could scratch one into flame. The herd would slow as it drew near the wash. The lead steers would be reluctant to make the short leap down onto the sandy floor but pressure from those behind would force them on. When they began that hesitation—that was the moment to light the powder strings and set off the blasts.

Two more punchers loped by, riding ahead of the herd, making certain of the course they were taking. One raised up in his stirrups, motioned to his partner.

"Got to keep them critters coming in slanchways! This here's where they've got to cross. They try somewheres else we're liable to have a bunch of them down with busted legs!"

Both galloped off toward the still growing sound and the dust cloud now beginning to hang over the flat.

Tom, paying little attention to the throbbing in his thigh, drew himself erect in order to see beyond the rim of the arroyo. The first of the steers were in sight, coming up at a jog, heads bobbing rhythmically. It was like a restless wave of brown, white, tan, and black funneling into a point aimed directly at him and the men nearby.

Another rider raced into view, hat hanging from its throat string and slapping against his shoulders. Honeymaker wondered if the men they'd left trussed in the Diamond G bunkhouse had been missed yet, and if their absence was making any difference.

Insofar as the herd was concerned, apparently not, he concluded. Cobb had gotten the cattle underway pretty much on schedule. It could be later on when—

A line of steers broke through the dust, suddenly pulling to a sliding halt at the edge of the arroyo. Wall-eyed, heads low, front legs planted stubbornly in the grassy soil, they began to draw back, mill.

"Now!" Tom shouted, and struck his match.

Dropping it into the strip of powder, he watched the bit of fire sputter briefly, catch with a spurt of yellow smoke, and then become a sizzling blue flame surging across the floor of the wash.

Glancing to left and then right, he made certain the remaining fuse strings were alight, came quickly to his feet, wheeled, and began to run toward the waiting horses securely tied to a stout piñon tree a short distance away. From the corners of his eyes he could see Quinn and the others hurrying to catch up.

A dozen paces short of the piñon the first of the powder cans let go with a mighty roar, releasing a rush of wind with the sound. Tom saw the bed of the arroyo rise in sheets of whirling dust, sand, weeds, brush, and other debris. Through it all he could hear the bawling of the cattle, and as he halted beside the frightened horses, and with the crew, sought to quiet them, he could see the mass of color shifting. Several steers were crowded over the rim, were thrashing about wildly on the floor of the arroyo still boiling with dust now blending with smoke from numerous fires ignited by the explosions.

"There they go!" Archer sang out.

Panic had spread like a flood through the herd, and as the front-running animals finally succeeded in turning, those behind them wheeled also, and suddenly all of the cattle were moving away, gathering speed as they pounded blindly into the opposite direction.

Gunshots, faint popping sounds barely audible above the increasing thunder of hoofs, began to echo as the riders sought to halt the fear-crazed steers, but their efforts would be futile; the herd would run for miles.

"Mount up," Tom said crisply, pleased and yet sobered by what they had done, and swung onto the saddle.

The others complied and all rode up out of the slight swale in which they'd halted, and struck a line for the ranch. On the first low crest, Honeymaker looked back. Layers of drifting dust hung over the rapidly vanishing herd, and two riderless horses were trotting aimlessly along the rim of the arroyo.

He shook his head. Likely there would be more than two men dead before the day was past if Kanin and Mayo did not give it up at this setback in their plans. They now had that choice; whether they would take it or not was yet to be learned.

He brought his attention again to the trail. The wooded

area where he'd told Tolliver, falsely, that he and the Diamond G crew would be waiting in ambush, was coming into view on his right. By cutting diagonally through it they could save a good five miles of the return trip, although the horses would be slowed somewhat by the heavy brush. He was anxious to reach the ranch as soon as possible, get set in the event an attack came.

Pearly Quinn kneed his mount in beside him. Strung out in single file behind were the rest of the crew. The cook's seamy face was wreathed in a wide smile.

"Them cows—they ain't going to stop 'til dark, way they was going!"

Tom grinned back. "That's what we wanted."

"Plan of your'n sure did work fine."

"It's not over yet," Honeymaker warned.

They had reached the first of the cottonwoods, and the horses were slowing, breaking stride as they began to enter the dense grove. A thought came to Tom. He started to turn, speak to Quinn. A splatter of gunshots broke out, coming from both the left and the right.

He saw Quinn flinch, and heard the clipping sound of bullets slicing through the foliage all around him. A moment later he caught sight of Henry Kanin and a dozen riders rushing toward him.

21

"Run for it!" Tom shouted, and whipping up his pistol, spurred straight for the nearest rider.

The puncher swung away. Honeymaker snapped a shot at him, veered in behind a thick clump of chokecherry. Guns were crackling all around him and smoke was beginning to hang in lazy layers between the trees.

He wheeled again, cutting sharp to his left. Another rider broke into the clear ahead of him. Tolliver . . . He snapped a bullet at the man, saw him sag as his horse rushed on. Elsewhere punchers were ducking in and out of the shadows, racing down the short, narrow lanes between the cottonwoods, firing steadily.

Honeymaker caught a glimpse of Heston. He was crouched low, almost flat on his saddle, coolly triggering his weapon at someone hidden from view. Roweling the buckskin, Tom urged him toward a thick stand of oak brush where the shooting seemed to be concentrated. He looked about anxiously for Quinn. The cook had been hit during those first moments when Kanin and his crew had surprised them. Just how bad Quinn's wound was he'd been unable to tell.

Two men hove into his line of sight—one of them being Joe Kanin. They were gone before he could fire. Tom swore, rode on. The hammer of guns was now a continuing, rolling echo, and dust, lifted by the horses' driving hoofs, was mingling with smoke and creating a thick haze that made visibility difficult.

Kanin had listened to Tolliver, that was evident, but Tom realized he had misjudged the rancher's reaction. He had expected him, with assistance from Mayo, to ride out ahead of the herd, and clear the way of any ambush. Instead Henry had taken a dozen riders and moved into the grove during the early hours of the morning and had laid his own ambush for the Diamond G crew, the arrival of which he probably figured would be around sunrise. Both he and Kanin had made a mistake, Tom thought wryly, but the end result was the same, nevertheless.

A puncher whipped by, head thrown forward, pistol gripped in his hand . . . Joe Kanin again . . . Honeymaker instantly swerved in pursuit, came head on into Quinn cutting across a small clearing.

"Pearly!"

The cook, left arm hanging, limply at his side, hawk features strained and coldly definite in the murk, jerked about, faced him.

"You all right, boy?"

Tom fought to keep the nervous buckskin from shying away, nodded. "You hit bad?"

"Well, I been hurt worse—"

"Doubt that!" Honeymaker shouted. "Start working toward the ranch. Too many of them for us. Pass the word."

"Sure," the old cook replied, and rode on into a pocket of sunlight filled with spinning particles of dust.

Kanin, with the large number of men at his disposal, could throw a noose about the Diamond G crew, close in, and have them in a trap; that probability had dawned on Tom and he was taking steps to prevent it. Their one avenue out was to keep moving toward the upper end of the grove.

"Jim!" he called, as Heston wheeled by him a dozen paces to the left.

The elderly cowhand swerved in to him. He was covered with a film of gray dust. Sweat stained his shirt and his eyes were red-rimmed and looked deep set.

"Head for the ranch—we can't buck these odds!"

Heston bobbed to indicate his understanding, swung his horse about, and hurried off into the trees.

The shooting had slackened somewhat, due no doubt to the thick, choking dust and smoke haze that was hanging in the grove like a solid wall. It was a bit of good luck for them, Tom realized, since it would mask their movements, make escape easier.

Weaving in and out of the dense growth, he searched for Archer and the vaquero. They could have received word to fall back from Quinn, but there was no way to be certain, and until he saw them, knew for sure they were pulling out, he could not leave.

A sudden spurt of gunshots behind him shattered the lull. He pivoted the buckskin, driving toward the source. A man riding a horse with Mayo's Walking M brand on its shoulder, broke out of the haze. Surprise blanked the puncher's face. He threw up his gun fast, wilted on the saddle as Honeymaker triggered his weapon first. Immediately Archer hove into view. He was leaning to one side, thumbing fresh cartridges into the cylinder of his weapon.

"Give it up—head for the ranch!" Tom shouted. "Where's Tularosa?"

Archer jerked a thumb toward an almost obscured stand of wild olive. "In there—last time I seen him."

Honeymaker spurred off for the tangled, thorny growth. His own forty-five was near empty, he reckoned, and switching it to his left hand, began to punch out the empty casings. He had one bullet left in the circle of six chambers, grinned tightly as he considered what it would have meant had he not thought to reload.

Gun filled, he rushed on, aiming for the point where Archer had said he'd seen the vaquero. Again the shooting had ceased. Sudden fear filled Honeymaker. Kanin and his men could have ganged up on the Mexican.

Three Box K hands rode across an open space to his right. All were looking straight on, oblivious to his presence. He let them pass, continued, smarting eyes switching back and forth as he strained to catch sight of Tularosa. The other members of the crew—Quinn, Heston, and Gabe Archer—were now on their way to the ranch; he needed only to get word to the vaquero.

A riderless horse trotted by, stirrups flapping loosely against its belly. It wasn't a Diamond G mount, he noted with relief, bore instead Con Mayo's mark—the second one he'd seen with the Walking M brand.

Both ranchers were in on the trap, that was evident. He guessed that knowledge shouldn't come as a surprise, and he supposed he had not thought much about Mayo since there'd been no sign of him. Like as not he was among the riders there in the grove and he had just failed to spot him.

Another spurt of gunshots rattled noisily behind him; Archer or one of the others of his crew fighting his way north. In the next instant Tom pulled up short as two riders cut in on him from the side. His jaw tightened. It was Henry Kanin and a man he did not know.

The rancher hauled back, features taut. "Get him!" he shouted. "Get him—goddammit!"

Honeymaker spurred in behind a thick-trunked cottonwood, pivoted, gun leveled. A third rider surged out of the brush toward him as he came about.

"*Patrón—quedado!*"

It was Tularosa and at the vaquero's shouted warning, Tom veered once more. He had a quick glimpse of Tularosa racing across the open, of Kanin and the man with him, and yet another Box K rider rushing toward him, guns raised; and then the small clearing echoed with the blasts of weapons.

Honeymaker saw the vaquero jolt, rock back on his saddle as he took bullets that were meant for him. On beyond the Mexican Henry Kanin was sliding from his horse, going to the ground.

Tom snapped a shot at the two Box K riders. Both swung away as he fired again, and roweling the buckskin, he moved up quickly to the vaquero. Seizing the reins of the sorrel the Mexican was riding, he wheeled, driving for the brush.

"Hang on!" he shouted, glancing back at the vaquero.

Tularosa, both hands locked to the saddle horn, grinned, made no reply.

Honeymaker did not slow the headlong pace, but kept the buckskin running hard with the sorrel, long head extended, neck pulled straight as he fought the leathers gripped tight by Tom.

Two punchers appeared, moving like shadows in the shifting dust and smoke. Honeymaker cast an anxious look at them. He would have to let the buckskin run on his own since he'd need one hand for his gun; he would not release the sorrel carrying Tularosa no matter what developed. A moment later he took a deeper breath. It was Archer and Jim Heston.

"Keep going!" yelled the latter. "Gabe and me'll hold them off!"

Honeymaker rode on through the now thinning grove. In another few yards they would break out of the trees entirely and enter a shallow valley that extended for a mile or so. The ranch lay just beyond its end.

He glanced back at Tularosa. The vaquero still clung to the horn but his dark face was shining with sweat and had taken on a pinched look.

"Hang on, *compadre*," Tom murmured.

Gunshots flatted hollowly above the drumming of the horses' hoofs. They came from behind—and not too distant. Kanin and Mayo's men were in pursuit. Archer and Jim Heston were doing all they could to keep them back.

They rushed down into the valley. At once the buckskin, unhampered now by brush and trees, lengthened his stride. The sorrel, too, finally accustomed to being led, began to run free. A rider appeared on the horizon ahead. It was Pearly Quinn. Honeymaker heaved a sigh. All of the crew were accounted for; two were wounded but alive—so far.

He felt his hopes rise higher as he topped out the upper rim of the little valley and saw the ranch below. It would be only minutes now. He looked back. Heston and Archer were coming on at a hard gallop, the Box K and Walking M riders just beginning to stream out of the grove. He grinned at the vaquero.

"We made it, *amigo!*"

Tularosa returned his shout with a weak smile, his eyes dull and set as they hurried across the flat separating them from the ranch house.

Quinn was at the hitchrack dismounting stiffly as Tom swept up with the sorrel in tow. Pulling up to the rail, he came off the buckskin in a long jump. Pain roared through him as his weight came down on his wounded leg, brought a curse to his taut lips, but he did not stop, hurried to the sorrel. Reaching up, he pried the vaquero's hands from the saddle horn, lifted him from the horse. Quinn moved up to help. He brushed the older man off.

"Get the door open," he snapped, and cradling the Mexican's slight figure in his arms, started toward the house at a halting run.

A stride or two in front of him he saw Quinn slow, hand drop for the weapon holstered at his side. The door was opening. A gust of anger and frustration rocked Tom. Kanin had stationed men inside the house, waiting for him. He allowed the vaquero to sag away from him. Supporting him only with his left arm, he reached for his weapon to back Quinn. A hard smile then cracked his lips as the thick panel swung wide and a slim figure stepped out onto the porch.

It was Ellie.

22

A second wave of anger pushed through Tom as he stepped up onto the porch; the girl had disobeyed him, had exposed herself to danger. Jaw set, he carried the vaquero into the house, and crossing to his own room, laid him on the bed.

"I'll look after him," Ellie said quietly at his shoulder.

He wheeled. Her eyes met the accusation in his. "I was worried about you—about what could happen, so I came here to wait," she said.

"Was a damn fool thing to do!" he snarled. "You could have gotten yourself shot—killed!"

"So could you," the girl said evenly, and bent over the vaquero.

Honeymaker gave her a brief, exasperated look, pivoted and hurried back into the adjoining room, once the kitchen of the house but in latter years serving as a sort of catch-all and storage area. Heston and Archer were just coming in, and beyond them in the yard the horses were trotting toward the corrals. There was no sign of Mayo or Kanin's men.

He paused beside Pearly Quinn. The cook was in the center of the room. He'd removed his jacket and the sleeve of his linsey-woolsey shirt was stiff with blood.

"Get in there and let Ellie fix that up," he said, pointing at the bedroom.

Pearly nodded woodenly. "The vaquero, he—"

"Took a couple of bullets that were meant for me," Tom said in a tight voice. "And he shot down Henry Kanin. Don't know if he killed him or not but—"

"Tularosa's dead."

At Ellie's soft words Honeymaker looked down. A tremendous weight seemed to settle upon him, crushing him, squeezing out some of his own life, supplanting it with bitterness and a cold hatred. The vaquero had been more than a friend; he'd been confidant, teacher, confessor—the father Burl Honeymaker never was.

"Goddamn them to hell!" he grated, fists clenching.

Ellie's voice, calm, businesslike, cut into his consciousness.

"I've got to clean your arm first, Pearly."

Tom turned away then, hiding his grief while within him anger was crystallizing into a hard, pitiless core of resolution. There had been a stubborn determination before but it was falling far short of the ruthless fury that now gripped him.

"Here they come," Jim Heston drawled, much as he might note the arrival of visiting friends. Blood stained the cloth of his jacket, too, but the wound was apparently of a minor nature and causing him little if any pain.

"Reckon there just ain't time to mess with this here arm now, ma'am," he heard Pearly Quinn say as he stepped quickly to the door. "It'll have to wait."

"But the bone's broken! You can't—"

"Ain't nothing bothering my trigger finger," the cook replied laconically.

Leaving the heavy panel open a narrow crack, Honey-maker glanced out into the yard. A half a dozen or more men had ridden in and were pulling up behind the bunk-house.

"One of them's going to find them yahoos we've got trussed up inside," Archer muttered. "Means we'll be fight-ing that many more. . . . Why'n the hell couldn't they've picked the barn to hide in?"

Gunshots broke out immediately, and bullets began to thud into the thick walls of the house. Glass shattered into a myriad of flying splinters and pieces as one of the marksmen concentrated on the window.

"Saves me knocking it out," Archer commented dryly, and resting the barrel of his pistol on the sill, pressed off six shots in rapid succession at the shadowy figures on the far side of the hard-pack.

"There they go—"

Tom, in the act of clearing off the table once used for kitchen purposes and dragging it into the center of the room where their supply of weapons and ammunition could be placed, turned again to the crack in the door. Two riders were ducking into the bunkhouse. The men inside had made their presence known in some manner and at-tracted the attention of their friends.

"We've got their artillery," Heston said. "Reckon that'll cramp their style a mite."

"Plenty of rifles waiting for them," Archer said.

The old puncher was right. Most men carried a pistol on their hips, a rifle on their saddles. The freed prisoners would not lack for weapons.

Honeymaker resumed his chore, and when the table was where it suited him, he piled the belts and guns taken from the six Kanin cowhands onto it, added two rifles that were standing in a corner, and a half box of cartridges for them that was on a shelf. Stepping then into the bedroom, he relieved the vaquero of his pistol and belt of ammunition.

He paused for a moment fondling the long-barreled weapon with its ornate, silver-inlaid handles, remembering how big and heavy it had seemed to him when he was a small boy, and how it had been that first time Tularosa had permitted him to fire it. The gun had all but jumped out of his hands. . . . When this was all over—and if he was still alive—the vaquero's pistol would find a place of honor on the wall where it could serve as a reminder of their friendship.

With that thought he thrust the pistol under his waistband, and adding the brass-studded belt to the others on the table, crossed again to the doorway and peered out into the yard. He was strangely silent, he knew, and Quinn and the others would be wondering about it, but he felt drained of talk, wanting only to get it all settled.

The riders were still gathered near and behind the bunkhouse, careful as always to take advantage of the shrubbery and not make of themselves a target while they seemingly awaited orders from someone. The prisoners had been delivered from bondage, evidently having left the crew's quarters by the rear door, as the party appeared to now be larger.

"What the hell they stalling around for?" Archer demanded peevishly. He was standing close to the shattered window, pistol ready.

Quinn, finally convinced by Ellie that he should allow her to treat his arm, was hunched in a chair. The girl had cut away the sleeve of his shirt, and using water from the bucket kept handy for drinking, had cleansed the wound and was wrapping a bandage around it. Setting the broken bone would have to come later.

"Holding back for Kanin or Mayo to tell them what they're to do," the cook mumbled.

"Liable to be a long wait if they're figuring on Kanin," Heston said. "Tularosa plugged him, Tom was saying."

"Fire—they're setting a fire!"

At Archer's shout Honeymaker jerked the door open a bit wider. Someone, not visible to him, had tossed a torch against the side of the barn. The flames were licking hungrily at the dry, weathered wood, and a scatter of last winter's leaves, bits of trash and weeds blown into the yard and deposited close to the wall, was already burning.

"That's what they're aiming to do," Archer said in a strained voice. "Figure there ain't a chance of getting us while we're in here 'cause bullets just won't go through the thick walls—but they can burn us out."

"Still got to get up to where they can throw a torch," Heston said, "and we can sure keep them from doing that—leastwise until dark."

"Well, they better not get no fire going in that tool shed," Quinn drawled. "There's aplenty of that blasting powder in there. They set it off they'll blow themselves to kingdom come!"

"Which I'll be taking as a mighty big favor," Heston added.

Tom watched the flames catch and start to climb the wall of the barn. Smoke was coming from the inside of the structure and the sounds of the frantic livestock trapped within were becoming louder. He swore deeply; there was nothing they could do about it—just as they would be unable to prevent Kanin and Mayo's men from putting the torch to the main house once night closed in. Abruptly he turned to Ellie. She had finished with Pearly Quinn, was gathering up the remainder of the cloth she'd found and torn into strips for bandages.

"I want you out of here," he said, taking her by the arm and propelling her toward the office in the front of the house. "You can slip away while they're all ganged up there in the back. Later on they'll surround the place and you won't have the chance."

"No, Tom, I won't—"

"We can't get a horse for you," he continued, ignoring her protests, "but you can make it to that patch of trees outside the gate and—"

Ellie reached up, laid her fingers upon his lips. "You're only wasting breath," she said, halting. "I won't leave—not as long as you're here. . . . Besides, I'll be needed."

She paused, frowning as guns began to hammer in the yard. Honeymaker studied her uptilted face for a moment and nodded in acquiescence. He wheeled and hurried back to where his crew, standing at the window and the partly open door, were laying down an answering fire. Drawing his weapon, he stepped in behind Heston, who dropped to his knees, making room for him at the narrow space between the heavy door and its frame, and added his efforts to theirs. The entire front of the barn was now ablaze and smoke was beginning to hang over the yard.

"Somebody ride in?" he asked when a lull came in the shooting.

"Didn't see nobody," Heston replied. "They just up and started blasting away at us."

"Somebody coming now," Archer said. "A whole passel of them."

In two long strides Tom crossed to the window where he could be afforded a broader view of the hard-pack. A grimness stiffened him. There were at least a dozen men in the group—and added to those already gathered near the bunkhouse, the odds—

"Honeymaker!" a voice shouted above the crackling of the flames, "hold your fire!"

23

"Some kind of a danged trick," Archer muttered. "Best we all watch close."

Tom moved up close to the jagged opening in the window. "All right—talk!"

At once the party of newcomers rode out from the smoky shadows near the corrals and advanced into the center of the yard, halting again when they reached the area fronting the house. Those near the crew's quarters began to appear cautiously.

"It's Joe Kanin," Heston said. "Expect that's his pa he's got slung across that horse he's trailing."

Tularosa's bullet had killed Henry Kanin. Tom hadn't been sure at the time, but it was definite now. Cold, unfeeling, he fixed his eyes on the younger Kanin. There was no pity, no sympathy in his heart, only a dull hatred and a pressing need for vengeance. It could only be better if a bullet from his own gun had cut down the rancher; then it would be a matter of sons having killed each other's father—a sort of poetic justice.

"I'm calling this off," Joe shouted, raising his voice to be heard above the raging fire. "Pa's dead. No sense in going on."

Anger ripped through Honeymaker. "*You're* calling it

off!" he yelled scornfully. "Like hell you are! We've got something to settle yet—you and me!"

Kanin stared in silence toward the window for a long minute. Then, "Don't know what you mean. Doing all this was Pa's idea—his and Con Mayo's."

"Not what I'm talking about. You killed my pa—put a bullet in his back. I'm going to make you pay for that!"

Tom, his voice throbbing, felt a hand on his arm. He glanced around. It was Ellie, appeal in her eyes. He shook her off, letting the soaring fury within him have its strong way.

"You're wrong, Tom," Joe Kanin said. "It wasn't me. I had nothing to do—"

"Don't try lying out of it!"

"I'm not, and if you're thinking you seen me—"

"Never said I did; I only know that it all adds up to you. You wasn't with your pa the day mine was bush-whacked, and that's not usual. And yesterday when some-body tried to put a bullet in me you were supposed to be working cows—over where nobody would notice whether you were or not. I figure it was you laying for me."

"I was with the herd yesterday," Kanin said doggedly. "You've got to believe that, Tom, because it's the truth."

"I don't have to believe a goddam thing that's not a fact—especially when I know better!"

Honeymaker paused, aware suddenly that Quinn and the others in the room, including Ellie, were staring at him in a strange, wondering sort of way. He had a quick wish that Tularosa was there, quietly standing by him, backing him, lending advice. But that was not possible;

the vaquero was dead, too—dead at the hands of the Kanins.

"You got anything else to say?" he demanded, his voice now cold.

Joe Kanin shrugged. A man near him spoke up. "Ain't no use trying to talk to him. He's just like old Burl—can't tell him nothing he don't want to hear."

"Maybe," Honeymaker snapped. "What kind of a horse are you riding?"

Kanin dropped the reins of the animal he was leading, rode a short distance nearer, and swung his mount broadside. It was a tan and black paint with a few white markings.

"What about yesterday? Was it a bay with one white stocking?"

"Rode this same one."

Tom shook his head, unconvinced. "Expect there's somebody that'll back that up."

"Hands I was working with will."

"Only natural they'd do just that," Tom said, his tone sarcastic. "They draw their pay from you."

Again Joe Kanin stirred. "You wanted proof. I give it but you don't want to accept it," he said heavily. "Ain't much else I—"

"You talking about a bay gelding with one white stocking?"

Tom swung his attention to one of the riders that made up the party at the bunkhouse. The roaring sound of the flames consuming the barn had tapered off, and the screams of the trapped livestock had ceased, the animals having escaped by the rear door of the structure. The heat in

155

the yard was intense and several men were stamping out small spot fires started by flying sparks here and there.

"What I said."

The rider backtracked to the bunkhouse, disappeared beyond it, and returned shortly leading a horse. He brought it to where Joe Kanin had halted.

"This here the one?"

It was the same bay, there was no doubt. Honeymaker's eyes narrowed as he settled his attention on the man.

"That's the one. Who're you?"

"Langdon . . . Jess Langdon."

The name was unfamiliar to Tom, one he'd never heard mentioned, but there were riders who worked for his father that he'd never known. Turning aside, he asked his question of the men in the room.

"Anybody know him?"

"Ain't never seen him before," Quinn answered at once.

Heston and Archer echoed his words. Honeymaker came back to Langdon. "That horse yours?"

"Riding him, that's all. Roped him out of the string this morning."

"Whose string?"

"The Walking M's . . . Con Mayo's."

Tom drew up slowly. "Who was riding him yesterday?"

The only sound in the yard was the crackling of the flames steadily devouring the last of the barn. Langdon shrugged and shook his head.

"Was Con hisself."

24

Con Mayo!

The anger within Honeymaker did not diminish, simply transferred its glowing ferocity from its believed objective to another—the correct one. It simply made no difference; Kanin or Mayo it was all the same. Likely both had been behind the bushwhacking, it had just been Mayo who pulled the trigger—and now would pay for doing so.

He had to admit, however, that Con was low on his list of suspects. That he should not have been was apparent now for he had stood at the end of the porch and heard Henry Kanin ask his foreman, Lou Cobb, about Mayo's absence and failure to take a hand in getting the cattle ready to move. He should have realized then that the Walking M owner was the one out to silence him—a desperate attempt to do so before he could talk or exact vengeance.

"Where's Mayo now?" he asked tautly.

Kanin was turning away, taking up the reins of the horse carrying the body of his father. Other men near the bunkhouse were mounting up, preparing to ride.

Langdon swung onto the bay. "Coming here, I reckon. Leastwise, he told us he'd meet us here."

"Tom . . . let the sheriff handle this," Ellie said quietly.

Honeymaker, stone cold and rigid, continued to stare

through the shattered window. "My job," he said bluntly. "Not leaving it to somebody else."

"It's not your job—it's one for the law!"

Joe Kanin and his crew were filing slowly out of the yard. Several other riders, Mayo punchers he guessed, while in the saddle, still lingered near the bunkhouse. He shook his head impatiently.

"I can't settle for that, Ellie—and you know I won't! Mayo's got to pay. I can't let any man get by with what he's done."

"And so you'll keep this terrible thing going on in the valley just like your father did!" the girl cried helplessly. "Nothing's ever finished, just violence following violence, killing following killing!"

"Know what I've got to do," Tom replied woodenly. "Mayo's coming here, and I'll settle with him. If you don't want to see it, get on your horse and—"

His words broke off. Three men were riding onto the hard-pack, slanting toward those near the crew's quarters. Honeymaker's mouth tightened. One of the new arrivals was Mayo.

"Con!" he called harshly.

The rancher halted, said something to the men who had been waiting for him. He got his reply, wheeled slowly, and rode to the center of the yard.

"Get off that horse!" Tom ordered, and moved toward the door.

Mayo dismounted, his lean shape somehow appearing heavier in the smoky murk.

"Cover me," Honeymaker snapped, and stepped out onto the porch. Facing the rancher, he holstered his pistol. "You're all done. I know it was you that shot Pa."

Mayo, legs spread, arms folded, head thrown forward, smiled bleakly. "Bull . . . you're guessing—"

"No, was you that put a bullet in his back, all right, then took a shot at me later on, figuring to wipe us out altogether."

"Talking—that's all you're doing—"

"Wrong again. When I said I had a hunch who did it, you lost your nerve, tried to ambush me. Tried again yesterday when you were supposed to be working your herd. You made a mistake there; I got a good look at your horse. . . . That enough or you want to hear more?"

Con Mayo had drawn himself up to his full height. He threw a quick glance over his shoulder at the men behind him.

"Don't look for any help from them. My crew's got them covered. This is between you and me—the last Honeymaker. Henry Kanin's dead, so if you get me, you won't have any more problems here in the valley. You can run things to suit yourself."

Mayo did not stir, simply stared at Tom.

"It won't be easy this time. I'm not turning my back on you like Pa did. You ready to—"

"All right!" the rancher shouted, abruptly finding his voice. "Maybe it was me. I was trying to talk to him, make him see he was hogging the range. He wouldn't listen, just laughed in my face. When he turned around and rode off, I grabbed up my rifle—and shot him. It was me after you, too. Figured I had to get you before you went to the sheriff."

"Draw—" Tom said coldly.

"Ain't about to! I heard what you done to Bill Jacks— and I'll tell you this. You gun me down you'll answer to my brother! He'll be getting here in the next few days and he'll look you up!"

"I'll be waiting for him," Honeymaker said evenly. "If you don't draw that gun, I'll start shooting anyway."

He heard a sound at the door behind him but did not take his eyes from the rancher. It was Ellie.

"Tom—please don't!"

The girl's voice was low, pleading. From the window Pearly Quinn's voice came to him.

"Listen to her, son. Been nothing but killings and such ever since your pa come to this country. Ain't proud to say that, but it's a fact. Don't keep it going—let it end right here."

Unmoved, Honeymaker shook his head slowly.

"You always set big store by Tularosa. Was he here he'd tell you the same thing. He hated your pa and only reason he stayed around was you. Revenging old Burl ain't going to be worth the price you'll be paying when you start walking around in his boots."

"Pa was murdered—shot down in cold blood—"

"Ain't denying that," Pearly said gently, "but who'd you best blame for it happening? Mayo, because he was the one that pulled the trigger, or your pa, because he drove him to it?"

"Tom—please—for our sake!"

Honeymaker gave no sign that he heard the girl's plea or the words that Quinn had spoken. Tense, hand hovering over the pistol at his hip, he continued to stare at the rancher, who appeared trapped like some wild thing.

And then Tom Honeymaker's rigid shape broke slightly. His shoulders lowered and the hard planes of his face, with their small, glistening patches of sweat, relented.

Without realizing it he had become another Burl Honey-maker, and that was something he'd sworn would never come to pass; he was not his father's son in that sense of the meaning—he was his own man.

"You'll answer to the law, Con, for killing Pa. What they do to you for that is up to them."

A small cry broke from Ellie's lips and he turned to her. "For everybody's sake, it ends here," he said, taking her in his arms.

DATE DUE

GAYLORD			PRINTED IN U.S.A.